I CARRIED THE HORN

I CARRIED THE HORN

Christine Pullein-Thompson

Allen Junior Fiction

I CARRIED THE HORN was first published by William Collins Sons & Co. Ltd. in 1951
White Lion Edition 1977
Revised Allen Junior Fiction edition 1900

British Library Cataloguing in Publication Data
Pullein-Thompson, Christine, *1930* –
I carried the horn.
Rev. ed
I. Title
823.914

ISBN 0-85131.517-8

ONE

Laurence had already returned when I arrived home from school. I could hear him whistling as I ran up the garden path. I found him in the stable grooming Overture, his fifteen-hands-two dark-brown hunter mare.

We were both just back from school for the summer holidays—Laurence from boarding-school, myself from the girls' day school in Chidlington—and before I go any further I think I had better tell you a little more about us.

Laurence and I live at Little Hall, a rambling red brick house, built on a hillside. Below us is the Days' farm and behind and to the right of us is Allate, a little grey village with a green and a bakery and tall trees.

The Days are great friends of ours. Together we hunt and own the Chill Valley Hounds. Andrew, the eldest of the Days (not counting Mr. and Mrs.), is huntsman; Valentine, next in age, is secretary; Kate and I whip-in and Laurence is field-master. The Days have a younger brother called Harry, who is eight and very sporting, but too young to be a hunt servant, much to his annoyance.

"I've raced you this time," said Laurence, grinning at me. "I was home by three. I say, Overture does look fit; you must have put an awful lot of work into her."

"Not much, really," I answered, recalling early morning rides, twilight rides and long hours with the body-brush. I looked at Daystar, who had been munching a feed, but who now was gazing towards the house, her large kind eyes alight with curiosity. I followed her gaze and saw Quinky our black cocker spaniel happily engaged in separating the contents of the dustbin into edible and non-edible.

"I caught them both," said Laurence, alluding to the horses. "I thought we could ride down to the Days" immediately after tea. By the way, what's this about Bank Holiday? I rang them up as soon as I got home; but only Kate was there, and you know what she's like on the telephone. Are we really to parade hounds at a show on Bank Holiday?"

"Yes, we are," I answered, and I saw the crowd in my mind's eye, and the ring, and Andrew, in scarlet, riding his brown hunter, Mulligatawny, and Kate and I on our greys, Dusty and Daystar; and, somewhere in the background, Laurence immaculately turned out on a shining Overture. I saw hounds gambolling with waving sterns and a glint in their eyes. In my imagination I heard the gone-away and saw us all galloping round the ring. "Don't you think that it'll be tremendous fun?" I asked.

"It'll be a good advertisement," said Laurence. "That is, if everything goes to plan. But where is the show? I hope it is not too far away. Horse boxes cost such a lot and we would have to have two." I laughed, because Laurence is always thinking of money, and because it was a lovely day and the first day of the holidays. Then I told him all about the Bank Holiday show.

Half an hour later, when I had changed my school clothes for jodhpurs, Laurence and I were riding along the chalky track which leads to Long Chill Farm. On either side the wheat was green and gold. Above us Allate lay dreaming in the sun. Nearer the farm, the cows were leaving the milking sheds for dry fields. On the pond in front of the farmhouse Mrs. Day's white Aylesbury ducks were stationary.

"Nothing changes," said Laurence with satisfaction. "You leave, you come back and, except for the changing seasons, it's always the same."

"Look, they're waiting for us," I cried, seeing a little group of people standing together by the kennels. "They're all there. They must have news; something must have happened. Oh, I wonder what it is," I cried, urging Daystar into a trot.

"Probably Jemima's had piglets or they've just heard we've got an enormous overdraft at the bank," said Laurence.

"Much more likely they've heard from the Downshire or the Waynesborough Chase," I said. "Valentine wrote to them both about hounds at least a month ago."

We were within earshot of the Days now and they were running to meet us, and all shrieking "Hallo!" at once. Valentine had a letter in her hand and Harry was carrying one of Aurelias's ginger kittens.

"You can put your horses in any of the boxes,"

Valentine told us. "Ours are still out."

"And then for the tour of inspection," cried Kate. "Oh, do hurry up. I do want to know what Laurence thinks of all the improvements."

"Improvements?" exclaimed Laurence. "And I haven't heard a word about them. Sandy, you've been neglecting me."

"But you weren't meant to know," cried Kate. "It's a surprise."

We put Overture and Daystar into two of the Days' boxes and then we hurried into the kennel-yard. I knew all about the improvements: I had helped with the painting and had watched the new copper being put in one hot Saturday afternoon. So I wasn't surprised by what I saw; Laurence was quite overcome.

"But this is wonderful," he kept saying. "It all looks so smart; and I think the new copper's absolutely marvellous. Feeding will be easy now."

"Do you really think it's all right?" asked Andrew anxiously. "We did sort of discuss the whole scheme last holidays, if you remember. Do you think the green's dark enough? Are the cream doors okay? We thought cream would add an air of cleanliness to the yard."

I followed Laurence's eyes round the yard and remembered how it had looked a year ago—a long open shed, a shed for calves, six pigsties with a boiler-house attached and in the middle, mud. The floors of the buildings had been terrible then and most of the roofs leaked. A few more months and the yard would have been derelict.

Then I remembered it later, weeks later after days of toil, when the calf shed had become lodging-rooms with courts in front, and the boiler-house at the end had become a proper kennel boiler-house, and the floors were concreted and the roofs were mended and the centre of the yard was no longer muddy but smooth and gravelled. And now the yard of our dreams was in front of me. The pigsties had cream-painted doors and window frames and had been used for the bitches in whelp, and puppies during the summer; inside were benches and concrete floors and outside the walls round the runs were mended, so that now each sty had a court of its own. The inside of the boiler-house had been white-washed, the outside was green and cream. The lodging-rooms and courts glistened with fresh paint and, best of all, the long open shed had been halved and converted into a draw-yard and a feeding-yard, both of which could be entered either from the yard direct or from the lodging-rooms.

Laurence's enthusiasm had silenced everybody's fears.

"I wanted to put a notice in the lane, saying, DRIVE SLOWLY PLEASE, WARE HOUNDS. But everyone else said that you would object and that it was a waste of money, since hardly anyone comes down here and when they do the lane's so rough they have to drive slowly anyway," said Kate, addressing Laurence.

"It would be rather a waste of money," said Laurence. 'Especially when you think of all the other things we ought to buy."

"We are having one notice painted, though," said Valentine a trifle apologetically. "It's to go at the end of the lane by the notice saying Long Chill Farm. It's just a signpost, really, saying CHILL VALLEY HUNT KENNELS."

"It's a necessity, really," said Andrew, "especially if

we're going to have a meet here during the season."

"Which we must do," cried Kate, "because Dad's promised to give it and there's going to be cherry brandy, as well as hot wine and rum punch."

"Sounds wonderful," I said.

"Grand," said Laurence. "Let's hope we get lots more offers of the same sort."

"Mum's already thought of the most wonderful eats," said Kate.

We were standing together by the boiler-house. "Let's have a look at hounds," suggested Laurence, walking across to the lodging-room. "I say, they do look grand," he exclaimed a few seconds later. "Old Vampire looks a different hound. No one can say they're thin now."

"No, they're rather the other way if anything," said Andrew, sounding pleased. "But they'll soon fine down when we start hunting."

We talked to Valiant and Vampire, both seventh-season hounds which we had obtained from the Downshire Hunt nearly a year ago. They were pleased to see us and wanted to rest their paws on our shoulders.

"I'm afraid this'll be his last season," said Andrew, running his hand down Vampire's heavy jowl. "He's had his day, poor chap."

In the next court were Gladstone and Graceful, old friends, too, and Willing and Wasteful and little pied Dainty; and two younger hounds, Chastity and Charmer, who had been drafted to us during the season from a different pack. They all wanted to talk to Andrew, who knows hounds better than any of us. They pushed and shoved and when he bent down to look at a cut on Chastity's shoulder, they all tried to lick his face.

"I wish the puppies were still here," said Kate.

"Did Sandy tell you about the wonderful walks we found for them?" Valentine asked Laurence.

I think I had better explain that when Valentine said "walks" she wasn't using the word in its ordinary sense. She meant that we had found farmers and landowners who would look after the puppies until they were old enough to live with the rest of the pack and start their serious education. Laurence and I had wanted to walk a couple, but Daddy objected; he said that I already spent far too much time looking after the horses during term, without having to manage a couple of hound puppies as well.

"The Haywards took a couple and so did the Austin-Smiths," cried Kate.

"We'll have to ride round and see them now that the holidays have started and we'll have more time," said Andrew. "I've been wanting to for ages, but what with the haymaking and the improvements and everything else, I haven't had a moment."

"We'll have to start proper exercising this month, won't we?" I asked, recalling last August, and *Fifty Years a Huntsman* and its views on the subject.

"Yes, the sooner the better," said Andrew. "I only hope Dad doesn't decide to cut the barley this week."

He's sure to start the day the new hounds arrive," said Kate, before crying: "but no one's told Laurence and Sandy about the letter yet. And we were waiting especially to spread the good news. We are hopeless."

"And I've been holding the letter in may hand all the

time," said Valentine, unfolding a sheet of paper with a printed address at the top. "It's about new hounds," she told us. "You know we agreed that I should write to the Waynesborough Chase and the Downshire some time ago. Well, I did and to-day, at long last, I've had a reply from the Waynesborough. They've got three couple to draft, two couple of unentered and one second-season and one fifth-season hound. Then, right at the end of the letter, they say something rather funny about some which would do for a scratch pack or as drag hounds and, apparently, they all can be ours for nothing."

"But that's wonderful," said Laurence, obviously thinking of our bank balance. "Are you sure we really can have them all?"

"Well, here's the letter," said Valentine, handing it to him.

"Obviously they have something wrong with them," said Andrew. "Either they're old and decrepit or else, and I think more likely, they're babblers or run mute or confirmed sheep killers. We'll have to be very careful."

Laurence was reading the letter. "I see they want us to go over next week," he said. "Can we manage that?"

"I don't see why not," replied Valentine.

"We'll have to," said Andrew. "We must have more hounds by Bank Holiday. Five couple will look awfully few in the ring."

"What about the terriers?" I asked.

"We'd better collect them next week too," said Andrew.

"You mean the two Mrs. Simmons offered us?" asked Laurence, remembering a letter I had written to him. "What were they called?"

"Weeny and Teeny," cried Harry, appearing from nowhere with yet another of Aurelia's kittens in his arms. Laurence made a face.

"It's all right, they're only their kennel names," said Valentine. "We can call them what we like."

We left the kennels and, passing through a gate by the boiler-house, entered what the Days call the Top Meadow, where the horses were standing head to tail in the shade of a few beeches—Andrews ugly brown gelding, Mulligatawny; Valentine's chestnut, Golden Syrup; Kate's light grey, Dusty; and Pink Gin, Mr. Day's sensible roan hunter, whom Laurence had hunted during the last season, until our grandfather had suddenly given us Overture; and, of course, Harry's little Lollipop, fatter and rounder than ever and always boss of the party.

"One thing is, they're fitter than they were at this time a year ago," said Andrew, patting Mulligatawny's neck. "But their manes are a disgrace. We really must do something about them," he said, surveying the thick ragged and uneven mess, which had once been Mulligatawny‘s neatly pulled mane.

"I know, we are awful," said Valentine. "I'm sure no one else lets their manes get in such a state."

"Well, it's no good making a toil out of a pleasure," said Kate. "But I do hate pulling manes."

"Well, they'll have to be done next week whatever happens," said Valentine. "They can't possibly parade round a ring with their manes in their present state and they are quite unplaitable." Kate sighed.

"I shall have to help get supper in a minute," continued Valentine, looking at her watch. "Don't you think we ought to get next week settled—decide who's going to see the Waynesborough Chase hounds and when and how? Then I can write tonight and get everything fixed."

"Oh, bags me go," cried Kate.

"And me," cried Harry.

"And about collecting the terriers," continued Valentine. "The sooner we have them the better, I suppose."

"Yes, and the hounds," said Andrew. "We want them all to be used to us by Monday, or we'll have the dickens of a job. I'm not looking forward to the parade much anyway."

"Oh, I am," cried Kate. "I think it'll be terrific fun. I wish I was in scarlet, though; black looks so drab in the sun, not to mention the sun showing up the dust on one's coat."

"I don't think more than three of us had better go to the Waynesborough Chase Kennels," said Andrew. "We don't want to look like a school outing."

"I should think you and Laurence had better go," said Valentine.

"But Kate and I've bagged," cried Harry. "Why shouldn't we go? You never let me go anywhere."

"You're too young," said Andrew.

"Will I be any good, though?" asked Laurence. "I mean, I don't know much about hounds. Couldn't Valentine go? After all, she is secretary. It seems awful for me to arrive, having done no work since last holidays, and bag all the nice jobs."

"But the huntsman and Master always select the new hounds," said Valentine. "It's their job, not the secretary's."

"Valentine's quite right," said Andrew.

"But I'm only a field-master; doesn't that make a difference?" asked Laurence.

"Why can't the three of you go? Wouldn't that settle the matter?" I asked. "After all, you all look quite grown up, not like school children, anyway. We don't mind staying behind, do we, Kate?"

"Yes, I think that's the solution," said Andrew. "It's a pity we can't all go, but you must agree it would be rather an invasion."

"Yes," said Kate sadly.

"I knew you wouldn't let me go," cried Harry angrily. "It's jolly mean. You never let me do anything nice. Anybody would think I was a baby. I bet you did lots of nice things when you were eight," he said, glaring angrily at Andrew.

"Not any that we wouldn't let you do," replied Andrew.

"You shall choose the terriers," said Valentine, in time to stem the fast-approaching tears. "You and Kate and Andrew and Sandy, to make up for not choosing the new hounds."

"But they're chosen already," he said, wiping his nose with the back of his hand and sniffing. "We're having Teeny and Weeny."

"What's today, Friday?" asked Andrew. "That means we can't see the new hounds till Thursday."

"You mean my letter won't reach them till Monday?"

said Valentine. "But why shouldn't we ring up?"

"And go on Monday, you mean?" asked Andrew.

"Yes, and collect the terriers tomorrow, if Mrs. Simmons agrees," said Valentine.

"Perfect," said Andrew.

"I'll go in and ring them both," said Valentine.

"I'd better come too," said Andrew.

"So had I," said Kate. "I'll take down particulars. And hadn't Laurence better come, in case they ask to speak to the Master and if Laurence is coming, surely Sandy might as well come too."

So in the end we all followed Valentine to the dark corner in the hall where the Days' telephone lives. "Now, you're not to giggle," said Valentine. "Because if you start I shall, and that would be terribly undignified." She dialled the Waynesborough Chase Kennel number.

"Absolutely tragic," agreed Kate.

"And you're not to shriek either," Valentine told us, "or make rude remarks; remember they can probably hear every word."

"All right, teacher," said Kate, giggling.

"I hope this isn't going to cost us the earth," said Laurence. "How is our bank balance, by the way?"

"Ssh," hissed Valentine.

Then a voice said "Hallo," with an accent, which Andrew said was Lancashire. Valentine said: "This is the secretary of the Chill Valley Foxhounds speaking. I received a letter from you this morning concerning three couple of hounds you have available."

The man at the other end seemed to know all about the letter and about the hounds. Andrew said he must be the huntsman; Laurence thought he sounded much more like the Master and Kate said he was obviously a Master who hunted his own hounds. I said: "Why on earth didn't we look up the pack in *Baily's Hunting Directory*, then we'd know?"

And Kate said: "Because we're nitwits and always have been and always will be."

At that moment Valentine gave us all a furious glare and said into the telephone: "I'm so sorry. What did you say?"

Valentine made a great many inquiries about the way to the Waynesborough kennels and Kate took down the details. Then she promised that we would be there not later than three on Monday, and Laurence said: "This call is going to cost a fabulous amount." And Kate shouted: "Their names, their names, you haven't asked him what their names are."

Valentine said: "By the way, you didn't mention their names in your letter. What are they called?" The voice at the other end said: "Wait a moment," and gabbled off some names, but his accent was so strong, none of us could understand any of the names. We all agreed that one began with Ra, but Andrew said it was Rattler and Laurence said it was Rambler, and there we gave up. Valentine rang off. "That's settled," she said. "Monday between two and three. I thought we could eat lunch on the road. That was the huntsman I was speaking to; he kept talking about the hounds they're drafting, but you made such a row I couldn't hear a thing."

"Sorry," said Kate.

We discussed Monday and agreed that the landrover

should leave Long Chill Farm between half-past ten and eleven, so leaving a good three hours in which to drive the hundred and twenty miles to the Waynesborough Chase Kennels. Then Valentine rang up Mrs. Simmons, whom we know quite well, because she's one of our subscribers and hunts with us regularly. She is also a landowner and has offered to give meets from time to time.

Mrs. Simmons said that she would be delighted to see us on the morrow and then talked for ages about "her gee" and about Weeny and Teeny. When at last Valentine rang off, Laurence said that he and I must fly as we were already a quarter of an hour late for supper.

While we bridled Overture and Daystar, Laurence and I arranged to be at the kennels by half-past eight the next morning, so that we could help to get most of the work done by eleven.

Riding home was lovely. An evening breeze stirred the wheat and fanned our faces. Little Hall looked like a house from another world; behind it the fields rose blue and gold until they met the tall woods, gold, too, beneath the sinking sun.

The horses were fresh and Laurence and I found ourselves longing for the day when the wheat would be cut, and we would be able to gallop across endless stubble, instead of trotting sedately along the hard, sun-baked track.

TWO

Kate and Harry were washing down the courts when Laurence and I arrived at the kennels on Monday morning. Teeny and Weeny, re-christened Pick and Shovel, were playing in the yard.

"They seem to have settled down all right," I said, pointing to the terriers and remembering how miserable they had been after they arrived on Saturday. In the boiler-house Andrew was whistling. "Hallo," shouted Kate, advancing with a bucket in one hand. "Valentine's ill: she's got sunstroke from sitting in the sun yesterday without a hat."

"What bad luck," said Laurence and I at the same moment.

"She's got a temperature," shrieked Harry. "A thousand and one or something."

"Hallo, do I hear Sandy and Laurence?" asked Andrew, appearing from the boiler-house. "Isn't it bad luck about Valentine? It would happen to-day."

Kate put down the bucket she was carrying. "Andrew says you and I must toss up to decide who goes in her place," she told me. "I've got a coin, you call."

"What about Harry?" I asked.

"Too young," said Andrew, who had joined us.

"Why didn't you call?" said Kate angrily. "Now I've lost it and it was my lucky coin."

"I'll toss," said Andrew, delving in his pockets and fishing out ten pence. "Call," he said, balancing it on the side of one hand.

"Heads," said Kate.

I saw the Waynesborough Chase Kennels in my imagination: extensive courts and long, low red brick buildings with doors painted black. Then Andrew caught the coin, slapped it on his other hand, and called out: "Tails."

I felt pleased and then mean, when I remembered how much Kate wanted to go.

"Bad luck, Kate," said Andrew. I began to think of reasons why Kate should go instead of me. She had probably got up much earlier, she had already done hours of work, whereas I had only just arrived. I followed Andrew to the boiler-house and told him my views.

But he didn't agree. "Nonsense, you do as much as anyone,' he said. "Anyway, quite honestly, I'd rather you came. Kate's so reckless; ten to one she'd accept a sheep-killer as a present before I had time to stop her."

"But it seems awful that two Dashwoods should go and only one Day," I said. "Particularly as I went over to Mrs. Simmons' yesterday."

"Well, it's settled anyway," said Andrew, stirring the meat in one of the coppers.

Half an hour later, we were exercising hounds on

foot. We didn't take them far—just to the end of the lane and back. Then we fed them and Laurence and I rushed home to make ourselves respectable for our visit to the Waynesborough Chase Kennels.

At a quarter to eleven we heard the landrover's horn hooting as it came along the top road.

I was still making sandwiches and Laurence was straining coffee into a thermos, but, somehow, we were ready when Andrew and the landrover drew up outside Little Hall's front gate. We waved good-bye to Mummy, and the next moment we were travelling swiftly towards Chidlington.

"I've remembered the map, and Kate's rather illegible instructions," said Andrew, swinging right by Allate's small, grey church.

Andrew was wearing a riding-coat and breeches and boots. Laurence and I, after some discussion, had put on our corduroy trousers. All too soon Andrew and Laurence fell to discussing our bank balance. After our succesful hunt in the East Nightley country—when we killed a fox which had been slaughtering chickens by the dozen every night for weeks—several people had sent us large subscriptions. The money from them and the regular subscriptions, and the caps we had collected since, had amounted to just over one thousand pounds. But that was at the end of March and, though we had thought we were rich then and had all clapped loudly when Valentine announced the figure at a finance meeting, the pounds had dwindled considerably since then, until now Andrew said we had barely five hundred pounds in the bank. I thought that sounded quite a reasonable amount, though I couldn't understand how the rest had been spent, but Laurence didn't share my opinion. Andrew said that though it was certainly a ridiculously small amount on which to run a pack of foxhounds for three months, it should be enough. We had, he explained, several gallons of cod-liver oil in stock and a large quantity of oats; that left us with only small additional expenses like green vegetables until the kale was ready, charcoal, sulphur and disinfectants and antiseptics. We seemed to be getting a fairly steady supply of flesh from neighbouring farmers. Mr. Day would always let us have straw free of charge and had promised to let us have the rest of last year's kibbled oats if our store ran out before November.

But Laurence was not convinced. He said that it all sounded quite satisfactory, but he still thought we were cutting it rather fine.

I said: "I suppose we can always borrow money if we are stumped,' which shocked both Andrew and my brother. They told me how fatal it would be if the Long Chill Hunt was known to be in debt, how it would ruin our reputation, and they reminded me that we still owed Mr. Day the best part of thirty pounds, a debt which we must definitely pay off before another season started.

After that we travelled in silence for several miles. I thought of the days ahead: of galloping across wet fields with the wind and the rain in my face; of early mornings and the first grey light of dawn; of meets at remote cross-roads and coverts wet with dew; of large fields behind Laurence, and meets in front of Queen Anne houses, and the thrilling sound of the horn and long hacks home in the gathering dusk. It seemed dreadful that the whole of August must pass before we could even begin cub-hunting. Kate and I had both wanted to start before September, but Andrew had said that, while the wheat stood, hunting was out of the question. I looked out of the window and saw flat fields fenced by rails, ditched on both sides; and here and there a barbed-wire fence.

Andrew and Laurence were discussing the Waynesborough Chase. We had looked them up in *Baily's Hunting Directory*. This is what we had found: "*Hunt Uniform: Red. Joint Masters: Major Sunderland, J. Peters, Esq. Hon Sec.: Colonel T. Mundy* (and their addresses). *Huntsman,* 1990: *R. A. Edwards.* Then, after the whippers-in: 40 *couples, marked number in right ear.* Then the kennels' address and *Meet: Mon., Wed., Sat. Sub. minimum:* £300 single; £500 *family; cap* £20. And finally a description of the past season's sport and the country over which they hunted. We had all read it several times and we had decided that the Waynesborough Chase must be one of the smartest packs outside the shires. Valentine thought the hounds would be first class, and Kate said that Major Sunderland, J. Peters and R. A. Edwards would slap us on the shoulder and call Andrew and Laurence "my boy." We had discussed the description we would have in *Baily's Hunting Directory* when the Chill Valley Foxhounds were officially recognised.

We returned to the subject now as we drove still deeper into the flat, unsheltered countryside.

"We'll have scarlet instead of red," said Andrew. "I think it sounds much more dashing."

"How on earth will we describe the country?" I

wanted to know.

"An up and down country with long gallops and varied fences and a plentiful supply of foxes," said Andrew.

"If only it was bigger," said Laurence. "I mean, lots of packs put, situated between, and then dozens of towns, or part of such and such a county. We can only put between Chidlington and Hettington, Flosshire."

"Perhaps the East Nightley will give us a piece of their country one day," said Andrew. We were silent for a moment. Then Laurence said, smoothing down his hair as he spoke: "I do hope Kate's wrong and they don't realise I'm only seventeen. It's rather humiliating for a Master to be addressed as my boy, or worse still, son."

"Oh, you're all right. Let's stop here for lunch," said Andrew, turning down a side road.

We ate our sandwiches on a grass verge in the sun. We were within ten miles of the Waynesborough Chase Kennels now and I couldn't help feeling excited. Andrew and Laurence seemed rather keyed up too. Laurence told me afterwards that he was wondering whether he should have come in a double-breasted brown suit—like he once had seen the Master of the Path Hill wearing—instead of just corduroy trousers and a hacking-jacket. We tried to remember all that we had read on the conformation of a foxhound. Of course, Andrew knew much the most. "*Good clean neck, well-laid and clean shoulders*," he said, quoting from The Book of the Foxhound.

"I'm hopeless on shoulders," said Laurence. "I never know a good shoulder on a horse when I see one, much less on a hound."

"*The forelegs should be straight with elbows set square,*" continued Andrew.

"And they mustn't be flat-sided or long in the back," I added, "or they'll have no staying power and a bad constitution."

"Both very bad faults for our kind of country," said Andrew. "Personally, I think an eye for a hound is rather like an eye for a horse," he continued. "It can only really be acquired by experience and by long hours spent gazing over the kennel door."

"Now I've finished with school, I shall be forever gazing over the kennel door, trying to find those *well-laid shoulders* which always elude me," said Laurence.

"We must make a real effort and go to Peterborough Show this year," said Andrew. "You'll see plenty of *well-laid and clean shoulders* there."

Peterborough, I think I had better explain, is the biggest foxhound show held in England.

"I'd love to go," I said. "Wouldn't it be wonderful if one of our puppies was good enough to compete?"

"Not likely, I'm afraid," said Andrew. "Foxhound breeding is very complicated and Valiant's not likely to give us a champion."

Laurence had stood up. "Isn't it time we took to the road again?" he asked. "It's nearly two o'clock."

"I hope we travel faster than ten miles an hour," said Andrew. "Still, better be early than late."

"We may not be able to find the kennels," said Laurence. "You never know, and it would be awful if we were late."

"Perfectly frightful," agreed Andrew, with a smile.

We clambered into the landrover again and sped on through the open countryside. There were few signs of habitation. Occasionally, we would pass a couple of cottages, and here and there a tree looking like a lost being in a strange land. We saw an occasional farm too, its red brick buildings close to the house. And though the countryside looked very picturesque now beneath the sun, I couldn't forget how cold and bleak it must be hunting, with no hills nor woods to break the fury of the east wind or lull the force of blinding sleet and rain. At the same time, I realised that it must be easier to stay with hounds, when so much land could be covered in one quick glance. Here, there need be no maddening gallops of a mile or more, to see but a couple of fields or a few more acres of woodland. And now, suddenly the landscape changed. We began to climb and the road twisted and we could see a gorse covert above us silhouetted against the sky.

Andrew changed down and said: "This must be one in six," alluding to the hill, I suppose. Then quite suddenly we were over the crest and the view below made Andrew stop, and Laurence and I hold our breath. More flat fields lay before us, but now they were intersected by streams and an occasional willow tree, and we could see an osier bed, like ours by the river Lapp. I suppose about ten square miles lay down there in front of us. In the distance we could see factory chimneys and the outlines of a town. Nearer were a few scattered farms, cottages and a Saxon church. And in the midst of it all, standing amid open fields, were the Waynesborough Chase kennels. They were built of red brick and in the shape of an L and, even from where we were, we could see two or three couple of hounds lying in the sun in a wired-in enclosure. Beyond the kennels stood an old red brick house, and midway between the house and the kennels was a stable-yard.

"Hunt stables, Master's house," said Andrew, pointing.

"What a wonderful preview," said Laurence.

"No difficulty in finding the Waynesborough Hunt Kennels," said Andrew, driving on down the hill, while every moment the landscape became clearer until suddenly we were on the flat again driving towards the village with a Saxon church. Soon, we turned left by a sign which directed us to the Waynesborough Chase Kennels and Laurence said: "I have a feeling we are beginning a new chapter in the annals of the Chill Valley Hunt."

I looked at myself in the mirror and saw a tangled mop of fairish hair. But by the time I had found my comb, which was under vast quantities of oats and bread in my trouser pocket, we had turned in between white gates and were fast approaching the kennels, and, since I was a whipper-in and whippers-in are not the sort of people who comb their hair in public, I hastily pushed my comb back into my pocket.

"It must cost thousands to keep up a hunt like this," said Laurence as we drew near.

"Well, after all, it is supposed to be one of the best packs outside the Shires," said Andrew. "I think weren't jolly lucky to be able to get hounds from them. I don't suppose they draft them to just anyone. And for goodness" sake be careful what you say. Remember, it's better to say too little than too much, and it's no earthly good pretending we know more than we do."

"Yes," said Laurence, and by the way he said it, I knew he was feeling hopelessly inadequate for the task ahead and much too young to be the Master of the Chill Valley Foxhounds. I determined to keep my mouth shut and say nothing to anyone, beyond good-afternoon or how do you do? Andrew looked determined and quite calm. His age might have been anything between seventeen and twenty-two—actually he was just eighteen. Laurence looked even younger than usual—about fifteen, I thought.

And now we had reached the gates into the yard.

"I think we'll leave the landrover outside," said Andrew, stopping and turning off the engine.

Laurence and I followed Andrew into the yard. We were met by a youngish man, who, after a few words with Andrew, vanished in search of the huntsman.

"A whipper-in, I should think," said Andrew. The yard looked very tidy: buckets were neatly upturned; brooms and shovels had been put away out of sight. "This is their quiet time," said Andrew. "I expect they're through now until they finish them off for the night." Coming across the yard was a small man wearing a cloth cap and breeches and gaiters.

"This must be him," said Andrew cheerfully.

"R. A. Edwards, huntsman, you mean?" I asked. Andrew nodded. Following the huntsman were a couple of terriers, rather like Pick and Shovel.

"Good-afternoon," said Andrew, and when Mr. Edwards answered we knew by his accent that he was the man Valentine had spoken to on the telephone.

"Pleased to meet you," he said, shaking us all by the hand. "So you've come to see some of our hounds." (I shall not attempt to reproduce his accent.) "Major Sunderland isn't over yet, but if you come with me, I'll show you what we've got." He called: "Bill," and the youngish man who had met us came sullenly across and together we visited all the lodging-rooms. The huntsman did no more than speak to hounds; if we admired one in particular he told Bill to fetch him out for our inspection. Hounds seemed very much alike, a few were darker than the others, but they were all more or less of the same height and all had considerably less white on them than any of ours at home. We had just reached the first of the hounds to be drafted — Tell Tale, True Love, Rattler and Rambler — when we heard a car stop and saw a large man, with grey hair and a grey moustache, step out of a tiny dark-red Fiat.

"Here's the Master," said R. A. Edwards, glancing significantly at Bill, as though to say, "and behave yourself or it'll be the sack for you." Bill looked slightly more sullen.

"Good-afternoon, gentlemen," said Major Sunderland. "I'm sorry if I've kept you waiting. What a wonderful day again." He shook hands with all of us. "Have you seen them?" he asked.

"I've shown them the lot, sir," said Mr. Edwards.

"What do you think?" Major Sunderland asked Laurence, waving a hand in the direction of True Love, Tell Tale, Rattler and Rambler. "They're the two couple of unentered ones."

"They look fine," said Laurence, looking helplessly at Andrew. "And very mature for their age" Andrew was talking to the huntsman and showed no sign of stopping.

"They're just what we're looking for," I said, forgetting my earlier resolution to keep my mouth shut. "I think they're beautifully put together," I continued, noticing True Love's short back and well-sprung ribs. "Our country's rather up and down, so we're particlarly anxious to acquire hounds which are well coupled-up." There I stopped abruptly, suddenly aware of how much I had said and wondering whether it had been too much. But Major Sunderland's next remark reassured me.

"Yes, they're grand fellows," he said, sounding pleased. "Come and look at the other couple. I'm sorry to see them go. One never has too many second-and third-season hounds. Or very rarely. But nowadays, with income tax what it is, one can't keep all one would like. You'll see these are darker than the others," he said a moment later, pointing to a couple in a lodging-room by themselves. "They both go back to Belvoir Vulcan. Here, Bill, come and fetch them out." When we had looked at Tomboy and Tempest for some time we all returned to the largest lodging-room and Bill called out Spendthrift, Ludlow and Conscript.

"I'm going to be quite honest with you about these hounds," said Major Sunderland. "A year or two ago we found we were very short of second-season hounds, and I imported several couple from other packs; among them were the couple and a half in front of you. As far as ordinary hunting goes, I have nothing to complain about; they throw their tongues well and they do their share, but they are, and so far we've been unable to cure them, cur dog hunters. Ludlow, over there," he said, pointing to the largest of them, injured a Pekinese only last week when out exercising and, of course, it caused the dickens of a row; we had the police round here and goodness knows what. Conscript and Spendthrift have only mauled a Corgi so far."

"I suppose they lead the other hounds astray?" said Andrew, who had been looking at Conscript.

"Well, they haven't to date," said Major Sunderland. "But I don't like to think what they'll teach the young hounds when they start coming out and quite apart from all that, I don't like the police popping round here every so often. It doesn't do the name of the hunt any good and it doesn't do fox-hunting any good; so if you'd like to take the couple and a half and see whether you can make anything of them, you're welcome. If they still go on the same, I think you had best knock them on the head. Personally, I believe once a killer always a killer. If I had had my way, they'd have been finished off months ago. We've been dillying and dallying over the matter far too long."

"Well, it's very kind of you, sir, to let us have them," said Andrew.

"Not at all," said Major Sunderland. "I'm delighted to see them go. I only hope they don't kill your neighbours' champion Pekinese or your most generous subscriber's pedigree Corgi."

"We'll be very careful," said Andrew. "We run our terriers with the pack and, I think, that may help."

Mr. Edwards had vanished. We could hear him reprimanding someone in the boiler-house. Major Sunderland invited us to tea, after which, he said, we could discuss the final details. I couldn't think of any final details to be discussed. But we all thanked him for the invitation and jumped into the landrover and followed the little red Fiat along the flat, straight drive which led to the old red brick house we had seen from the top of the hill.

Later we met Mrs. Sunderland, who was tall and grey-haired, and then we ate cucumber and egg sandwiches and some rather dry scones, in the garden beneath ancient cedars. A Dalmatian, a spaniel and a dachshund watched us hopefully while we ate, and the Dalmatian, who was called Roundsman, grabbed a scone out of Laurence's hand. When we had finished eating, the dogs had saucers of tea and the rest of the sandwiches.

Then Laurence and Andrew and Major Sunderland wandered into the house to discuss details and I was left with Mrs. Sunderland, who was nice but rather inquisitive. She asked me all about the Chill Valley Hunt and tried to find out Andrew's and Laurence's ages. But I paid no attention to her hints and, when she asked me point-blank I pretended not to hear.

When Andrew and Laurence returned, I knew by their faces that everything was all right. They were both smiling from ear to ear and Major Sunderland was laughing. And now the time had come to say goodbye. I stood up and, glancing across the open landscape, I saw cows going back to pasture and, along the straight flat roads, men bicycling home from work.

We thanked Mrs. Sunderland for the tea and then we shook hands with Major Sunderland and thanked him for the gift of Spendthrift, Ludlow and Conscript and for letting us have the other three couple—as well.

But Major Sunderland waved our thanks aside. "It's wonderful to find such young enthusiasts in these days of anti-blood sports bills and all the abominations of modern civilisation," he said. "I hope they do you credit and I hope that one day, when you can spare the time, you will come and enjoy a day in our country. Mr. Peters and I will always be delighted to see you."

We thanked Major Sunderland again and climbed into the landrover and drove away towards the kennels, shouting good-bye and waving frantically to Major and Mrs. Sunderland, who were standing together in front of the house.

"They're nice, aren't they?" I said.

"Very," said Laurence. "Do you realise he's let us have three couple of hounds!"

"Has he really?" I said, not surprised, because I knew it already.

"He's really keen on hunting, that's why," said Andrew. "If we want to get recognised next year, he says he'll speak for us when our pack comes up for the approval of the Masters of Foxhounds Association."

"Recognised? Why do we need to be recognised?" I asked. "Why aren't we all right as we are?"

"Because people can't qualify for point-to-points by coming out with us," answered Andrew. "Nor could we hold a point-to-point if we wanted to."

By now we had reached the kennels and this time the gates were open, so Andrew drove right into the yard. Our hounds were waiting in the draw-yard. First Bill and Mr. Edwards brought out Spendthrift, Conscript and Ludlow. They loaded without any fuss and Laurence and I helped Bill fetch the other three couple while Andrew talked to Mr. Edwards.

When all our hounds were safely in the landrover we shook Mr. Edwards and Bill by the hand, and Mr.

Edwards asked us to let him know how they settled down, and Bill wished us good luck and all the best. Then we drove away through the white gates and out towards the village with the Saxon church.

None of us spoke, except to hounds, until we were driving uphill again towards the gorse covert now crimson and gold beneath the sinking sun. Then we discussed the days ahead and Laurence took out his pocket diary and we planned future meets, and visits to farmers and expeditions to see Vagabond, Villain and Viking, Venus, Verger, Victor, Vanity and Vision—our puppies out at walk.

Five miles the wrong side of Chidlington we had a puncture. But it didn't seem to matter; we all felt so happy and within half an hour the wheel was changed and we were travelling swiftly towards Chidlington once more. Now we fell to discussing Valentine's and Kate's reactions when they saw how many hounds we had brought back with us. I said that they would both have a heart attack; Andrew thought Kate would have hysteria and Laurence said they wouldn't be able to speak for joy.

Hounds came to life when we reached Chidlington; they stood up and looked out of the windows at the queues in front of cinemas and the crowds on the bridge gazing into the river. Ludlow nearly had a fight with Tempest because they both wanted to look out of the same window at the same moment. Fortunately, Laurence and I took quick action and parted them while they were still only snarling with their hackles up. Nearly all Allate seemed asleep; a few lights gleamed from cottage windows and two men sat drinking outside the White Lion. Otherwise there was no sign of life, except for a couple of dogs setting out for a hunting expedition, who shied into the ditch when our headlights swept round a bend in the road.

It was nearly dark when we turned down the lane to Long Chill Farm. The lights were on in the farmhouse and we could just see Valentine, Kate and Harry waiting by the kennel-yard gate. They were waving frantically and we waved back and shrieked, "Whoo-whoop, wind 'im," which drove the hounds in the back of the landrover into a frenzy. When we had calmed them we put our thumbs up and Kate gave a view holloa and hounds in kennel began to howl, Tempest nearly jumped through a window and in the top meadow one of the horses neighed. Mr. and Mrs. Day came out of the farmhouse and told Kate she would wake the whole neighbourhood with her holloas. Andrew stopped the landrover and we all stepped out. A few more minutes and the new hounds were in the lodging-room Valentine and Kate had prepared for them, and Andrew, Laurence and I were answering an avalanche of questions. But at last there was silence. We turned off the boiler-house light and Andrew said he would run Laurence and me home, and Kate said she would come too.

The church clock at Allate struck twelve as Laurence and I crossed the lawn on tiptoe and crept into the kitchen. We found shepherd's pie and treacle tart waiting for us in the simmering oven. On the dresser there was a note which read:

"You're much too late
For us to wait
Any longer.
Quinky's fed
And safe in bed
And we're asleep
So please creep."

Then: "Hope you had a good day; don't stay up too long talking. The water's hot if you want a bath." Then Mummy's and Daddy's initials.

"What nice parents we have," I said.

"Ssh," said Laurence. "Dont't talk so loud, you'll wake them up."

But Laurence's warning was unnecessary, for at that moment we heard the stairs creak and a few seconds later Mummy appeared in her dressing-gown and her bedroom slippers.

THREE

Tuesday dawned fine. We introduced the new hounds to the rest of the pack and then, rather cautiously, to Pick and Shovel. Tempest growled at Vampire, but Vampire stood his ground and no fight ensued. Ludlow was the only one who paid any attention to the terriers and when he looked at them, Andrew rated him loudly and after that he looked the other way.

We coupled most of the new hounds together and took the whole pack out exercising on foot quite successfully. In the evening we rode. That night Andrew put the new hounds in the largest lodging-room with the rest of the pack. He slept on a camp-bed next door and when a fight started soon after midnight he was ready. He was wakened twice more, and but for him True Love might well have been killed by the rest of the pack.

Next day we rose early and exercised hounds and horses together. The weather had changed during the night and it was a wild and windy morning. Daystar was very fresh; she jogged and pulled and was so ill-mannered that I determined to school her on the morrow. Overture did not behave much better and Dusty barged into Golden Syrup when Kate cracked her whip.

"This looks grand for Bank Holiday," said Andrew sarcastically, riding sensible Mulligatawny in one hand. "Why don't you exercise them some more?" Andrew's remedy is always exercise as far as horses' manners are concerned. He likes to ride in an egg-butt snaffle and a martingale; if a horse pulls a lot, he says he needs more exercise and if he pulls only a little he says he's keen.

"Well, Dusty's had as much exercise as Mulligatawny," retorted Kate angrily. "More, actually, because I took her out the day you went to the Waynesborough Chase kennels."

We had been riding through woods and now, as we turned and started to descend into the valley, a hare got up right in front of the pack.

"'Ware riot. Hold up, hold up together," shouted Andrew.

"Hold up there, hold up together," I yelled, urging Daystar into a gallop as hounds streamed away in full cry towards the farmhouse.

"Stop them before they reach the wheat," yelled Andrew. "For the love of——" The rest was lost in the wind. I could hear Kate quarrelling with Dusty, who didn't want to leave the other horses. Ahead was wheat, acres and acres of it, golden and green. I gave Daystar her head and we seemed to cross a stretch of fresh stubble in an incredibly short time. But we were too late. In spite of my cries and my ineffective attempts at whip-cracking, the hare dived into the wheat and hounds after her. Now, not daring to ride through Mr. Day's wheat, there was little I could do until the hare broke out into the open again. Valentine and Laurence were galloping to the far side. Soon, they each stationed themselves at a corner and Kate was already at the third. Andrew was blowing a series of discords on the horn and calling: "Come away back home; come away, come away back home," only it didn't sound quite like that.

Hounds crashed backwards and forwards through the wheat giving tongue at intervals. I rode round the outside cracking my whip and halloaing and then, quite suddenly, they started to return. First, Gladsome and Vampire then, to my surprise, Ludlow and Conscript, and soon, slowly but surely, all the others, except for True Love who continued to hunt rabbits industriously amid the wheat.

"We'd better leave him," said Andrew, turning Mulligatawny's head for home. "He'll come on in a moment."

"I'm sorry I was too late," I apologised.

"It's Dad's special crop, that's the worst of it," said Andrew. "We'll hear something when we get home."

"Was he looking then?" I asked.

Andrew pointed, and I saw Mr. Day standing by the milking sheds. "He saw it all," said Andrew.

"Won't it stand up again?" I asked, looking at the patches of battered wheat.

"I'm afraid it's too ripe for that," said Andrew. "One consolation is, it won't be here much longer. A few more weeks and the main of it will be carried."

"It'll be awful if they behave like that on Bank

Holiday," said Kate, joining us on a sweating Dusty. "How on earth will we keep them in the ring?"

"The crowd round the outside will help," said Andrew. "If I remember rightly, hundreds go to the Chidlington Show. Last year they had the East Nightley, but once was enough for them—too much trouble dressing up and getting hounds there, I expect, and probably the horses had to come in specially."

I felt worried as we rode on down to the farm. I had been looking forward to Bank Holiday, but now I saw a thousand complications—would hounds behave or would they vanish into tea-tents, disappear into the crowd or get killed by cars or lost in the midst of the fair? How would Daystar behave? It would be her second visit to a show, and at the first she and I had disgraced ourselves. I saw myself pursuing hounds backwards and forwards through a seething mass of people, among roundabouts and swing-boats, over guy-ropes and round innumerable tents, on a madly excited Daystar, while the loudspeaker announced the Chill Valley Foxhounds and the crowd at the ringside waited. I saw disaster ahead or, at least, disgrace. And there are only four more days, I thought, and once again I determined to school Daystar on the morrow.

"Here comes True Love," said Kate. "Forrard on to him, forrard on." We had reached the kennels.

"Six, seven, eight and a half; all on," said Andrew, counting hounds as he let them into the draw-yard.

On the way home I told Laurence of my fears for Bank Holiday; only to find that his were still more alarming. For the rest of the week they hung over us, and the days passed all too quickly. Wednesday,

Thursday, Friday and Saturday they came and passed, without leaving us a spare moment and soon, too soon, Sunday arrived, a wet Sunday I shall never forget.

Up to this moment the Days had remained remarkably calm. Laurence and I had said nothing of our fears, and in the rush and bustle of the last few days no one had noticed our glum faces. Now, suddenly, the Days began to dread the morrow. Kate was certain Dusty would refuse to enter the ring, Andrew was convinced that he would be unable to blow the horn at the crucial moment. It was as though they were seeing the display through Laurence's and my eyes for the first time. Valentine became irritable; Harry did nothing but ask questions; Kate rushed from the stables to the kennels, from the kennels to the house and back again, forgetting why she had come and where she was going. Hounds were upset by the atmosphere and Conscript nearly killed True Love, which upset Andrew who had been the calmest of the Days up till then.

Fortunately, towards evening, the Days became too weary to be cross any more. Laurence and I helped them clean their boots, brush hounds and put grooming tools ready for the morrow. We all became very silly. Andrew said that we would put up the best display ever seen this side of Bankley; Valentine said that hundreds of the crowd would rush forward and press generous donations into our ever-open palms; Kate said that the show committee would present us with a cheque for fifty pounds "just to pay expenses, don't you know?" Laurence said that we would be photographed and that we would all smile at the right moment, the horses would have their ears forward, and hounds would be looking lovely and the photograph would be so wonderful that it would be put on the front page of *Horse and Hound*, on the back of *The Times*, in the middle of the *Daily Telegraph*, in the local papers, and in *Riding* and *Pony*. I just imagined a complimentary column about us in the local papers on the following Saturday. In the end it was nearly eleven when Laurence and I crawled into bed to dream of reporters, photographers, tea-tents, upset prams and of all the catastrophes which might occur on the morrow.

When the alarm clock went off at half-past four the next morning, I wakened with a feeling of approaching disaster. For a moment I couldn't collect my wits, then I remembered that today was Bank Holiday, that today we were to parade round a ring, in front of hundreds of people, with our hounds and our ring-shy horses. I switched off the alarm and wondered why we had ever accepted the invitation. At that moment I would have done anything to be able to shut my eyes and go to sleep again. But I thought of the Days, probably already up and, jumping out of bed, I rushed to Laurence's room.

As usual, Laurence took ages to waken. He's maddening in the early morning; he sleeps half-way down his bed and you have to shout or he doesn't hear you. Even if he isn't asleep he pretends to be.

On this particular morning I shouted: "Wake up, it's Bank Holiday," and then: "Wake up. It's half-past four and we're parading with hounds at Chidlington today." In reply Laurence groaned and pulled the bedclothes still farther over his head. I suddenly felt very angry. I was shivering in my pyjamas.

"Will you wake up?" I cried, seizing Laurence by the shoulder and shaking him roughly. "I believe you've been awake all the time," I cried when Laurence wailed:

"Why can't you leave me alone?"

At that moment Daddy arrived. He was wearing a dark-green dressing-gown and his hair was all on end. He was obviously angry. Laurence sat up and pushed his hair out of his eyes. "What *do* you think you're doing making such an unearthly row in the middle of the night?" demanded Daddy. "Even if you can't sleep and must get up at this ridiculuous hour because you're performing at some ridiculuous show in Chidlington during the afternoon, you might show some consideration for others. I thought, at least, you were being murdered, by the noise."

"Sorry," I said.

"It was my fault really," said Laurence.

"What's the matter?" called Mummy.

"There you are," said Daddy . "Now you've wakened your mother up. You really are inconsiderate children. Why you have to get up at this ridiculous hour I can't imagine."

I said "sorry" again, and so did Laurence. Daddy said: "Well, you might try to be a little more considerate in future." I said: "Yes, I will." Then I dashed back to my bedroom to dress. A few seconds later I charged straight into Laurence, who was at the head of the stairs, and we both crashed downstairs together. It was Mummy who came to our rescue this time. She thought that the house had collapsed on us and was amazed to see us standing holding our heads in the hall. We explained what had happened and then we dashed into the kitchen, and, then out to the stable.

Overture and Daystar were both lying down. They whinnied when they saw us and stood up and blinked at the lights we switched on. We refilled their water buckets and fetched their feeds and the haynets we had filled the night before. Then I washed Daystar where she was dirty, and Laurence started to groom Overture. By six o'clock they were both looking lovely and, after eating a hurried breakfast, we plaited their manes, which took us till half-past eight. After that we took our parents their early-morning cups of tea and then we started for Long Chill Farm. We had left our hunting-clothes with the Days the evening before, so that this morning we would be able to help get hounds ready and then change afterwards. Already the day was hot. A bright sun shone out of a cloudless sky and any trace of yesterday's rain had vanished.

Overture and Daystar were fresh. They jogged and shied, and shook their heads at the hundreds of flies already swarming over us.

We found all the work done at Long Chill Farm. The Days, like us, had risen at half-past four. Andrew and Valentine had washed down the kennel courts, and Kate and Harry had groomed Mulligatawny and washed, groomed and plaited Dusty. They were all looking very smug when we arrived.

"Everything's done!" cried Kate.

"Aren't we clever?" shouted Harry.

"It seems Daddy was right," said Laurence. "I can't think why the Days must always get up so madly early."

"They like to be on the safe side," I said.

"We can't possibly start before twelve," said

Andrew, as Laurence and I halted our horses outside the kennel-yard gate "We haven't got to parade till three and it's certainly not more than a couple of hours' hack from here."

"We are mad," said Kate happily. "I can't imagine why we got up so early."

"Nor can I," said Laurence rather sourly.

"I'm going to help Bert Saunders," cried Harry. "He's getting Meadowsweet ready. He says I can ride over with him in the wagon if I'm quiet and remember to wash my face."

Meadowsweet is the Days' grey Shire mare. She was competing in the heavy turn-out class at three-thirty. We put Overture and Daystar into boxes, then Kate and I followed Harry. We found Bert Saunders busy plaiting Meadowsweet's mane. He said that, except for her mane, she was ready. Meanwhile, Andrew and Laurence had vanished on an errand for Mr. Day. Kate and I polished the horses for some time; then we dressed, which took ages, because we were both out of practice and couldn't tie our hunting-ties. By the time we were ready, Andrew and Laurence had returned, and while they dressed we drank tea and ate hot lardy cake in the Days' kitchen.

At twelve o'clock exactly, Kate, Andrew, Laurence and I were mounted in the yard. Andrew gave the okay. Valentine opened the draw-yard gate and nine couple of smiling hounds burst out into the sunlight.

It was very hot riding beneath the August sun in full hunting kit. We felt stifled inside our black coats, our hunting-ties, our breeches and our boots. We had left our gloves with Valentine, who was coming over later with Mr. and Mrs. Day and Pick and Shovel, and we soon began to wish that we had left all our other hunting kit behind as well. We imagined the same ride in lightweight summer jodhpurs and cotton shirts and felt hotter than ever. Hounds' energy seemed unaffected by the heat. They gambolled joyfully ahead, upsetting dustbins, peeping into prams and dashing in and out of gardens. Andrew told me to ride ahead. "And don't let any of them past," he said.

By now we had reached the main Chidlington road and we were able to ride along a grass verge under trees for a mile or more. Charmer, Conscript and Tell Tale all tried to pass me at regular intervals. I managed to hit Conscript, and when I shouted at Charmer she turned back. But Tell Tale was not so easy; he gambolled past me again and again, and Andrew wouldn't let me hit him. "He's only young," he said. "He'll learn in time. If you hit him before he understands what you want, he'll be disheartened and then he'll never be any good."

Meanwhile, Kate was having trouble behind. Ludlow had found someone's lunch in a haversack under a tree. He was wolfing down cheese sandwiches at a terrific speed. Then Charmer saw a cat and oblivious of all traffic, she dashed across the road in front of a huge removal van, which swerved violently, narrowly avoiding a woman on a bicycle.

I shrieked, "Sorry," and cantered after Charmer, while Andrew shouted: "Go on, go on, don't stop." I decided Andrew was talking to the owner of the removal van. Charmer was looking up at the cat, now safely installed in the branches of a tree and I actually managed to hit her. Andrew apologised to the driver and the woman on the bicycle; Charmer rejoined the pack and we rode on.

"The first whip must ride on whatever happens," said Andrew, catching up and riding alongside me. "You see, if you're in the front and you stop, because, say, Charmer's chasing a cat, the whole pack stops and the next moment they're chasing the cat as well, whereas, if you ride on (*a*) the rest of the pack probably follows; (*b*) if they don't, the second whip has somebody to send them on to. Do you see what I mean?" he asked.

"I think so," I said. "I'm sorry about just now. I'll try to remember in future."

"That wasn't your fault," said Andrew, dropping behind again.

Several horse boxes passed us and we began to feel excited when we saw the suburbs of Chidlington ahead.

"Now we must keep the pack together at all costs," said Andrew. "If they start hunting a cat down the High Street, we've had it, and for goodness' sake keep your eyes open for dogs."

"Okay," I said, shortening my reins and imagining hounds in full cry in the middle of Chidlington.

"Thank goodness, the shops are shut," shouted Kate.

"Get over, get over together. Hup!" cried Andrew as a cattle truck and two horse boxes flashed by.

Now we had really reached the suburbs of Chidlington. Most of the gardens were empty, except for occasional sunbathers who sat up to watch us pass. They made us feel hotter than ever in our hunting kit, and as we rode over Chidlington bridge and entered the town proper, I longed to dive into the river Lapp and feel cool again.

We felt as though we belonged to another age as we rode down Chidlington High Street. On each side of us stone buildings rose up to the blue sky. There were no cars to be seen; all the shops were shut. At any moment we expected a hansom cab or a stagecoach to come clattering up the street. People stopped to watch us pass, and called out: "A-hunting we will go," and "Where's the fox?" and "What a pretty sight!" A young man made a rude comment.

Hounds were marvellous. They stayed together beautifully and, when I turned round in my saddle and looked back at them and at Andrew in his scarlet coat and Laurence and Kate on a prancing Overture and Dusty, I felt indescribably happy. Soon we reached the traffic lights and they were red. A small crowd collected while we waited, and back-chatted with Andrew. Then the lights changed, and we turned left and rode up Bell Street.

Daystar was enjoying herself. She's very vain and she loved leading the way. She carried her head and tail even higher than usual and though she didn't pull, she was full of impulsion and longing to gallop. When we came to the end of Bell Street we turned left again and saw Chidlington football ground ahead of us.

"Keep them well together," said Andrew as Tell Tale and Charmer surged forward. Soon we could see the ring. A jumping class was in progress. Scattered over the showground was a multitude of people. They stood ten deep at the ringside. There were swing-boats, but no roundabouts or bumper-cars, and a huge car park crammed full of cars, horse boxes and cattle trucks of every description.

"I had no idea it was such a big show," said Laurence. "What a pity we couldn't have had a practice at a little one first."

"Oh, I do feel awful," said Kate. "I'm sure I'm going to let everyone down."

"Don't be silly. Why should you?" said Andrew.

Hounds began to break apart as we entered the showground. Across the far side we could see a beer-tent and a couple of tea-tents.

"That's where they'll go," said Andrew, pointing.

"Where do we go now?" I asked, looking for a corner where we could hold up hounds.

"Over there by the trees," answered Andrew, pointing to a row of poplars beside a split-oak fence. I looked at my watch and saw there was half an hour before our parade. The sun was still beating down on us. It was perfect weather for the Bank Holiday crowd. We rode over to the trees and Valentine met us with a rubber and brushes. She was wearing linen trousers and an open-necked shirt and, I think, secretly, we all envied her.

Hounds were exhausted. One by one they collapsed in the meagre shade offered by the poplars. We dismounted and, taking off our coats, groomed our sweating horses and polished bits and stirrups and saddle-soaped our tack again. Valentine delivered scraps of information. "Shovel was sick coming over," she said. "There are lots of people we know here. One of the East Nightley subscribers won the hunter class with a horse called Fallen Idol."

"Poor Shovel," said Kate. "Good thing he wasn't sick over you."

"There were thirty-three entries in the jumping," Valentine continued, "and ten clear rounds. They're jumping-off now. When they've finished, it's the hackney class, and then it's us."

"Oh, dear, I do feel dreadful," wailed Kate.

"That means we had better get up in about twenty minutes," said Andrew. "Can everyone remember exactly what we're going to do?"

We had talked it all over before. For the last few days we had talked of little else.

"Yes, I lead in," I said. "I halt opposite the enclosure and you take off your cap, and we all bow. I lead round the ring, first at a walk, then at a trot and then at a canter. Then you blow the gone-away and we all gallop like anything about twice round, and then I pull up and we go into the middle again and salute."

"Then it's all over," said Kate, "and we collect our pack again, which probably vanished before we even started to trot."

"Don't be silly," said Andrew sharply. "Why should they vanish? If you feel like that, something's bound to go wrong. It's your job to keep the pack together."

"I'll stand by the entrance with a whip," said Valentine, "and try and stop them coming out."

"I shall be there too," said Laurence. "I'm only going to appear for the final salute."

"The crowd will keep them in round the sides," Valentine told Kate in soothing accents. "They're at least ten deep."

Kate said nothing. I knew she was dreading the next

hour and yet I'm sure she wouldn't have missed the parade for worlds. I felt near despair myself and, once again, I wondered why we had ever accepted the invitation.

Mr. Watson came across with a liver-and-white spaniel at his heels. I saw Andrew glance apprehensively at Ludlow, Conscript and Spendthrift, but they were too hot to feel like hunting cur dogs. They glanced at the spaniel and then looked away again.

Mr. Watson is our most sporting foot-follower. He will cover miles in the course of a hunt and generally sees more foxes than anyone.

He now saluted us and said, with a laugh: "Nice to see you again. Still going strong, I see. You've got some new hounds too; you shouldn't have brought them all that way, though. The hot roads will work havoc on their feet. They'll all be lame tomorrow, you'll see. Mind you pull up your girth before you go in," he told me, with another laugh. "It wouldn't do for your saddle to slip round in the ring."

As I had just loosened Daystar's girth I found Mr. Watson's advice rather annoying. Andrew was looking sullen. I don't think any of us were in the mood for criticism. We were all too hot and nerve-racked. Mr. Watson was looking us all over with a critical eye. An ill-adjusted spur, a garter the wrong way round, no such mistakes are missed by Mr. Watson. But this time he seemed satisfied.

"Not quite the weather for hunting kit," was all he said, with another laugh. Kate sighed with relief. Laurence winked at me. Andrew muttered: "Inspection over."

"But where are the terriers?" asked Mr. Watson. "I heard you'd bought a couple."

"They're still in the landrover," answered Valentine.

"They'll be in the parade," said Laurence.

"Would you like to come across and see them?" asked Valentine.

Valentine and Mr. Watson walked away across the showground together. "Nice to see old friends again," said Andrew.

"If only they didn't talk," said Kate.

"Don't be so temperamental," said Andrew.

"Here comes Colonel Hayward with Felicity and Patience, not to mention a couple of our young hounds," cried Laurence, sounding quite excited.

"Verger and Victor," said Andrew.

"I say, they have grown!" exclaimed Laurence. "I believe they're bigger than Chastity or Charmer already."

Colonel Hayward waved and his daughters ran towards us, towed by Victor and Verger.

We all shrieked "hallo," and Colonel Hayward shouted: "Not quite hunting weather." Felicity said: "Oh, don't pull so, Verger," in a whiny little voice. And Patience said: "Steady, Victor."

We all gasped as we looked at our couple of young hounds. They had grown enormously since the Easter holidays. They were already as large as their mother, Charmer. They had short, strong backs and cheerful, smiling faces. Verger, the darker of the two, had a white streak across his neck and a white splash on one side of his quarters. Victor was slightly taller with three white spots along his back and a white streak between his eyes. Both their sterns were tipped with white. "You've done them well, sir," said Andrew. "They look wonderful."

"To think that they are ours!" said Kate, turning to me with shining eyes. "More ours than any of the older hounds because we bred them—Chill Valley, Victor and Verger. Doesn't it sound lovely? Oh, I do think we're lucky. I'm sure they're much better looking than any of the older hounds."

Colonel Hayward was telling Andrew how his daughters exercised Victor and Verger when they were out riding; how Victor had stolen the Sunday joint one day and Verger had dug up the asparagus bed on another.

Felicity and Patience were talking to Laurence. I patted Verger's well-covered ribs and said to Kate: "Who knows, they may be good enough for Peterborough in spite of what Andrew says." As I spoke, I saw a future Peterborough in my imagination—Victor and Verger parading round the ring; scarlet coats; dozens of huntsmen, Masters, whippers-in, all talking hound, hound, hound. I heard congratulations and people asking where we came from and why they had never heard of us before.

"Only the hackneys now," said Kate, bringing me back to reality with a jerk.

Mummy and Daddy had arrived. I could see them parking the car. Mr. and Mrs. Day were giving Meadowsweet a last look over. She was magnificent with her gleaming, jingling brasses and her mane plaited with ribbons to match her blue and red farm-cart.

Another hour and it will all be over. We'll be hacking home through Chidlington, along the straight road to Allate and then down into the valley, I thought.

"We didn't bring Joke and Jester," Felicity told me, patting Daystar. "We thought the jumping would be too professional and there aren't any competitions."

"I'm not entering Daystar either," I said. "She's too big for the children's jumping by half an inch, and she can't jump high enough for the open."

The hackneys were lined up in the centre of the ring. A military band was playing the "March of Pomp and Circumstance." Valentine appeared with Pick and Shovel, and Andrew said: "Time to mount." Colonel Hayward said: "Best of luck." Felicity said: "We'll cheer you." And Patience said: "Hadn't we better put the pups back in the car?"

I looked at the crowds and my knees felt weak. When I was mounted my strength returned. Daystar was still full of energy. She didn't want to stand; she looked at the crowds and then started digging with all four feet at once. My boots felt tight and my hunting-tie, which I had industriously starched, was rubbing my neck. Valentine handed me my gloves. "Hold up, hold up together," cried Andrew as hounds suddenly came to life. "Keep an eye on Conscript," he told me, "else he'll be eating up someone's best French poodle."

Andrew's voice sounded strained. I suddenly realised that he was probably more nervous than any of us. A hunt can have incompetent whippers-in and still have a reasonable reputation. But no hunt with a hopeless huntsman can expect to exist for long.

"I'll do my best," I said, looking for French poodles at the ringside. The crowd still stood ten deep. The judges were conferring together.

"As soon as the hackneys start going round with their rosettes, we'll advance," Andrew told me.

"Hold up, hold up together. Stop him, Valentine," cried Kate as Conscript and Spendthrift made a dash and disappeared together in the direction of the tea-tent.

"Shall I go after them?" I asked, already urging Daystar forward.

"No, you stay here," said Andrew. "Valentine will fetch them back. You'd never find them in the crowd."

Laurence was talking to the host of people who had surrounded us. I heard the click of a camera; then a child began to cry and a woman cried angrily: "Get down, get down."

"Dad says you ought to be in the collecting ring by now,' cried Harry, tearing across the showground towards us. "Hurry, hurry, you're going to be late."

"Can't the child be quiet?" said Andrew angrily. "The whole show can hear every word he says."

"Shall we move on?" I asked.

I felt quite calm as I led the way towards the collecting ring. The hackneys were wearing their rosettes; they looked fantastic and frivolous as they trotted round the ring for the last time, while the crowd applauded. Daystar felt like bubbling over. She would only canter very slowly. I could hear Dusty playing up behind. Valentine returned from the tea-tent dragging Conscript and Spendthrift. "Am I hot?" she said.

"Try the same thing in hunting kit. Then you'll know how we feel," said Andrew.

"Shovel, Shove, Shove, Shovel, Shovel," called

Harry, chasing Shovel, who was fleeing towards the swing-boats, his tail between his legs.

Subconsciously I had halted. "Lead on, lead on!" cried Andrew. "Those who aren't present, can't parade."

"I'll catch him for you. Don't you worry," volunteered a little old man with a limp. "What is he, a Melrose?"

"That's right," said Andrew.

I saw True Love, out of the corner of my eye, vanishing towards the beer-tent as we neared the collecting ring. Mr. Watson was in close pursuit.

The loud-speaker announced: "A parade of the Chill Valley Foxhounds, by kind permission of the Master."

If we only we didn't all look so young, I thought, suddenly remembering our ages; I bet the crowd think we're a great joke. They were probably expecting the East Nightley with thirty couple of hounds, and everyone in scarlet.

"Sandy, lead on. What are you waiting for?" cried Andrew in an exasperated voice.

I used my legs much too hard and Daystar, who had been standing impatiently digging, dashed into the ring.

"Steady, not so fast," cried Andrew as loudly as he dared.

I led the way into the centre and halted opposite the grandstand. Then something very embarrassing happened. The loud-speaker said: "I think everyone here should know how the Chill Valley Foxhounds came into being." I caught Kate's eye and she made a grimace; neither of us knew what was coming next. I felt embarrassed standing in the centre of the ring with hundreds of eyes on me. Kate told me afterwards that she felt the same.

"It is not an old pack, in fact it's a very new pack," the loud-speaker continued. "The coming season will be only its second season. The hunt servants are all voluntary. The Master expects no guarantee. The pack you see in front of you now was started from scratch, literally scratch." Then the loud-speaker became even more embarrassing. It talked about our great enthusiasm and initiative, and made remarks which still make me blush when I recall them. Finally, it pointed out that we were all still in our teens, "which alone made us unique in the history of foxhunting."

There was a terrific burst of clapping when at last the loud-speaker was silent. Still in our teens, I thought, why did they have to say it? Hounds had been awed by the loud-speaker; clapping had the opposite effect; they dashed forward. "Lead on, lead on!" cried Andrew. Dusty was trying to gallop Kate out through the exit. I trotted on round the ring. Daystar felt like dynamite under me waiting to go off. I sat down and we cantered, and each time we passed round the ring there were more hounds by the ring ropes being fed and stroked by the crowd. Poor Kate was nearly frantic behind. I could hear her cracking her whip and crying, "Forrard, forrard on," and all the time Dusty was trying to leave the ring. We had cantered round twice and still Andrew hadn't blown the "gone-away." It was like a dreadful nightmare. I looked behind and saw that we had only three couple of hounds with us. The others were gobbling cake and sandwiches at the ringside or had vanished altogether. Andrew had the horn to his lips and suddenly the "gone-away" rang out across the showground and, as if by magic, hounds appeared from everywhere; they left their cakes and sandwiches, the tea-tent and the beer-tent, the prams and the multitudes of stroking hands, and in a matter of seconds we were galloping round the ring as though we would never stop with all hounds on. Someone gave a view halloa, and I heard someone say: "Well, they know their job all right." Then we were in the centre of the ring again and Andrew was taking off his hat and, suddenly, Laurence was with us too, looking worried and much too young for an M.F.H.

Then the crowd clapped for ages and I decided that they thought Kate and I were ten years old and Laurence thirteen, and were clapping because they thought we were infant prodigies.

Mr. and Mrs. Day, Colonel Hayward and his daughters, Mr. Watson, Mummy and Daddy, Valentine and Harry, were all waiting for us in the collecting ring. "Oh, dear!" said Kate. "Why must they all come just when I want to go away and hide my head for shame?"

"Good show, very good show," said Colonel Hayward.

"They looked a picture," said Mr. Day, Andrew said nothing. Kate was looking away across the showground. I wanted to say, I suppose you mean the horse show, to Colonel Hayward, though I knew he was alluding to our parade.

"An absolute picture," repeated Mr. Day, "and what a crowd!"

"Who wrote that miserable piece for the loudspeaker?" Laurence demanded angrily, his voice unusually loud.

"Ssh," said Mummy.

"What was wrong with it?" asked Mr. Day. "Bit of good propaganda." Laurence made a hopeless face at me.

"What, the bit about teenagers?" asked Andrew with a laugh. I suddenly wondered whether Mr. Day had given the show committee the details revealed by the loud-speaker. He is very proud of his children. Though he criticises them endlessly to their faces, he exaggerates their achievements out of all proportion, compares them favourably with all the other local children and boasts shamelessly about them outside his house. I could see him saying, "Hardly more than kids, they were, when they started; come to that, they're still all in their teens now," and then boasting of Andrew's prowess in the hunting-field, his vast knowledge of hounds; of Kate's fearlessness and of Valentine's sound business head.

"They will do it," I heard Mr. Watson say. "If there's a bit of cake about the beggars will have it."

"They looked lovely," Mummy told me, "and Daystar looked wonderful too."

"Aren't you blocking up the entrance rather?" asked Daddy anxiously. "There seem to be all sorts of carts and carriages wanting to come in."

"Heavy turnouts, you mean," cried Harry.

Colonel Hayward was patting Daystar. "She went very well," he said. "If you ever want a home for her, let me know. I shall have to get something bigger for the kids in a year or two."

"Now's your chance," said Daddy.

"No fear," I replied, introducing Colonel Hayward to my parents. "I'm going to keep her for ever and ever." As I spoke I tried to visualise hunting on a horse which wasn't Daystar.

"We'd better move on," said Andrew. "The turn-outs want to come in and I see a steward advancing."

We stayed to watch Meadowsweet win reserve in the class for Heavy Turnouts. Andrew was sunk in gloom. He said that we had failed. He had been unable to blow the "gone-away" at the right moment, hounds had misbehaved, Kate had been nearly galloped out of the ring every time we passed the exit and, finally, there had been the terrible remarks over the loud-speaker. Only once before had I seen Andrew so despondent, and that was in the early days of the Chill Valley Hunt, when we found that our hounds were to cost a fortune to feed and we had only a few pounds between us. Valentine said that Andrew was exaggerating. From the ringside it had looked a perfectly ordinary parade of foxhounds. Admittedly there were fewer hounds and fewer scarlet coats than usual, which took away a little of the glamour. But otherwise there was nothing noticeably unusual about the parade. No one had noticed how many times we galloped round before Andrew blew the "gone-away" Dusty's disgraceful display had only made the people admire Kate for her horsemanship, and although hounds had vanished it was only because the crowd preferred giving them cake to watching them parade.

Andrew said nothing, and Laurence said, "Where are the donations and the generous subscriptions we were expecting?" in a sarcastic voice.

I counted hounds and saw that they were all on.

"Perhaps they'll give us more now that they know we're all teenagers," said Andrew.

Valentine called Pick. "Shovel's in the landrover," she said.

"Home," said Andrew. "Thank goodness it's over."

"I'm dashed if I'll wear this coat home," said Laurence. "Or my gloves. I've had enough baking for one afternoon."

"Let's dump them all in the landrover," said Kate. "If you'll hold Dusty I'll take them across."

We felt much better without our coats, and when we reached the other side of Chidlington and saw our own familiar landscape, we began to feel quite cheerful.

"We've been spoilt, that's the trouble," said Kate. "We've never got over our success in the East Nightley country. Before then, we didn't expect to be taken seriously."

"But we're not a joke," said Andrew. "We've got perfectly good kennels and quite a decent pack of hounds. Why shouldn't we be taken seriously?"

"I wonder who told them our ages," said Laurence.

"To think how hard you've tried to look twenty!" I said, beginning to laugh.

"It's all very well for you, you're not an M.F.H.," said Laurence, beginning to laugh too. "Whippers-in are often quite young, but who's heard of a Master of under twenty?"

"Is there anything wrong in being unique?" I asked.

"Get over, get over together, hup!" cried Andrew as a lorry flashed by. "We'll have to start getting the puppies back before Christmas," he said.

We discussed the puppies and their various merits as we rode through the summer evening. When we reached the kennels, Laurence and I put our horses into loose boxes and helped the Days settle hounds for the night.

Then we rode home to a dinner of cold ham and salad and ice-cream. We expected our parents to be critical, but somehow they had missed our mistakes and in spite of all we said, they retired to bed still convinced that our parade had been a huge success.

FOUR

After the Bank Holiday show we could think of nothing but cub-hunting. We longed to see all the wheat cut on Long Chill Farm, so that we could once again draw Long Wood, Hazel Wood, Quarry Copse, Poacher's Copse and Badger's Wood. We bullied Mr. Day endlessly. But he only said: "Give us time. They haven't started cutting the wheat yet on the other side of the hill."

We were filled with energy. We rose at dawn to exercise hounds for hours and hours, exploring countryside hitherto unknown to us. We visited our puppy walkers and saw hounds which we hardly recognised as the puppies which had left us in the spring. We schooled our horses. We bought large quantities of whipcord to be used as lashes, and iodine pencils and whistles, which Andrew said he would hear more easily than Kate's and my unorthodox halloas.

Every day our hounds and horses grew fitter but still there was wheat standing on Long Chill Farm. In spare moments we made endless plans for the future, and

Andrew gave us lessons in blowing the horn. Kate confessed that she hated being first whipper-in and asked whether she might always be second. I questioned her and discovered that she found Andrew unnecessarily critical. "It's all very well for you," she said. "He's not your brother. But whenever I'm first whip, it's grumble, grumble, and I get in more and more of a muddle, and then I do something silly and he's cross. Honestly, I would much rather be second whip. I can be on my own then and I love riding on the down-wind side, even though I am in the right place when hounds turn only once in a blue moon."

I knew how Kate felt. Sometimes, I have a longing to be miles from everyone with the wind and the rain, or the sun and drifting clouds for company, and the landscape and my horse and the cry of hounds. To be alone with hounds, in the right place at the right time, is an achievement one never forgets. Everything seems worthwhile then; even those terrible moments of despair when hounds are running and the second whip has to stay back in covert trying to send on hounds which don't want to go.

But in a way I was pleased. I love being first whipper-in. You ride well forward then, assisting the huntsman across country, counting hounds as they come out of covert, but leaving the missing ones to the second whipper-in; you keep your eyes open for hounds hitting heelway or giving tongue to a hare. So I said: "Are you sure?" Kate said: "Yes." I said: "Well, it suits me." And so it was settled.

Mr. Watson was always turning up at the kennels during those hot, energetic August days. He helped to stir the puddings, the meat and the broth cooking in the coppers, and advised Andrew endlessly.

Felicity and Patience frequently joined us exercising. We liked having them because they didn't talk too much, and their ponies were sensible and completely hound-proof.

Gradually we began to know our hounds better. Conscript, Spendthrift and Ludlow improved and the better they came to know Pick and Shovel the less they looked at other dogs. Once or twice when Andrew was very busy helping on the farm, Valentine, Kate, Laurence and I took out hounds without him. We were very cautious then and somehow we managed to avoid catastrophe.

So September came and Mummy and Daddy left for a holiday in France, and Laurence and I did the housekeeping, assisted by Gladys and Aunt Sarah, who came to stay. We were very lazy about cooking and lived chiefly on ice-creams, biscuits and cheese, and awful meat pies bought from our butcher. Then, suddenly, Mr. Day announced that the corn was cut and that we could draw his coverts on the following Saturday. We all became wildly excited then. We groomed our horses for hours and the Days cleaned their tack for the first time since Bank Holiday.

We rang up a few people like the Haywards and Mr. Watson, and told them about the meet and they promised to tell other subscribers. We decided we would wear our boots and breeches but not our black coats. Andrew would of course be in scarlet. We exercised the horses for hours on Friday, but we left hounds in kennel so that they would be really lively on the morrow.

We had arranged the meet for six o'clock at the

kennels, so Laurence and I rose soon after four on Saturday morning. It was a perfect morning for cub-hunting—damp and misty with the promise of a fine day in the air.

All was ready when Laurence and I reached the kennels. There were four riders in the yard—Felicity, Patience, a girl called Jane Browne on a bay pony and a boy called Roger Wilcox riding a cob—and Mr. Watson. The Days were bringing their horses out of the stable, except for Andrew, who stood ready at the draw-yard door. They shouted, "Hallo," and then Andrew let hounds out, and Valentine handed him Mulligatawny, and the next moment we were riding through the mist towards Poacher's Copse. Daystar was just as fresh as usual, in spite of the hours of work I had given her the day before. But my schooling had certainly had some effect: she was much lighter in hand and though she wanted to gallop she didn't pull. Soon, Andrew sent me to the far side of Poacher's Copse with instructions to bang my saddle flaps and to hold up cubs, but to let an old fox go. As I galloped on, I wondered whether I could still tell the difference between an old fox and a cub; it seemed years since I had seen a fox of any description.

Poacher's Copse is half-way out of the valley. Out of it was wafted the smell of pine needles and damp leaves; somewhere in a tree a pigeon was saying: "My toe bleeds, Betty." I halted Daystar on the far side and she stood still with ears pricked. Soon I heard hounds put in, the horn and Andrew calling: "Leu in, leu in there." Then I saw a scarlet coat coming towards me through the mist. Tell Tale and True Love put up a rabbit, and for a moment there was a crash of music and Daystar threw up her head and twirled round. Then Andrew said: "You haven't seen anything, have you?" And I suddenly realised that I hadn't really been looking.

"No, nothing," I said, wondering whether other people's minds wandered as much as mine. Andrew blew hounds out and we rode on to Long Wood, where Andrew, once again, sent me to the far side.

There were plenty of cubs in Long Wood, and for nearly an hour hounds hunted them backwards and forwards through the thick undergrowth. I turned a brace of them back and so did Kate. Mr. Watson turned back a brace and a half. Then, soon after half-past seven, the sun broke through the early morning mist, we were too hot in our coats and scent became patchy. Tell Tale and True Love were still hunting rabbits most of the time, but Ludlow, Conscript, Tomboy and Tempest were hunting well and when the whole pack was in full cry the noise was terrific. Spendthrift seemed to be an individualist. He walked round outside the covert, sniffing at tufts of grass, but otherwise showing no intention of hunting. The morning became steadily hotter and by nine o'clock there was no scent at all, and Andrew decided to call it a day. I counted hounds and found that they were all on, and Andrew told Kate by blowing toot-ta-toot on his horn. Then we said good-bye and good-night—which sounded rather silly—to the Haywards, Jane Browne, Roger Wilcox and Mr. Watson. Patience and Felicity both thanked us for a lovely morning, but Jane Browne and Roger Wilcox just kicked their ponies and rode away towards Chidlington without a word.

We had a marvellous ride home; hounds gambolled on ahead and our horses walked sensibly with long loose reins. Down in the valley, the fields were dappled in the sunlight. Above, the sky was a cloudless blue.

Laurence said that the landscape was like a Van Gogh painting. Andrew disagreed. He said that he didn't know much about art, but he did know that Van Gogh had never painted hounds and that no painting of the English countryside was complete without a pack of hounds in the foreground. Valentine said: "Why must it be like anything? It's unique like the Chill Valley Hunt."

"You'll be saying it's teenage next," said Andrew.

I could see Aunt Sarah coming out of Little Hall, with a shopping-basket in one hand.

"I don't like cub-hunting much," said Harry. "It's so slow. We never had a gallop at all this morning."

Andrew gave his brother a long lecture. He said that you shouldn't like hunting only when there was galloping and jumping. You could get plenty of that in hunter trials, paper chases or with a drag hunt, and that if you took an interest in hound work you were never bored, not if there were a million mediocre days one after another. Harry looked disbelieving, and Laurence said: "How do you think hounds hunted today, Andrew?"

"Pretty well on the whole," said Andrew. "True Love and Tell Tale are not very steady; but they'll learn. They've got plenty of time yet."

"What about Spendthrift?" I asked.

"I don't think he'll ever be any good," said Andrew. "We had one like him with the Path Hill (the hunt to which Andrew whipped-in before he moved to Long Chill Farm), he was never any good. They shot him in the end."

We were all silent, thinking of Spendthrift's ultimate fate, unless he changed his mind and decided to hunt.

"It's awful the way you have to destroy hounds," said Kate at last. "It will be terrible when we have to start on Vampire and Gladsome because they've got too old."

"Well, they'll have had a good life," said Andrew.

We could see a lorry picking up the Days' milk-cans from the end of the lane.

"I'll have to leave you the feeding when we get back," Andrew told us. "I've promised Dad I'll be on the tractor to-day."

Laurence and I put our horses into loose boxes when we reached the farm. We helped Valentine and Kate feed hounds and wash down the courts. Then we rode home to a belated breakfast.

We cub-hunted again on the following Saturday and killed in Hazel Wood, which delighted Mr. Day, Bert Saunders and all the local farmers. Mrs. Simmons came out with us on that occasion and asked us to meet at her home on the following Saturday. We accepted the invitation, and, though the meet was to be at six-thirty, she said there would be eats and drinks for all.

We were all rather excited about the meet at Mrs. Simmons' house. She lives near Hettington and her coverts, many of which run down to the river Lapp, would be new to us. We were told that she had a whole litter of cubs in one covert and a host of old foxes scattered over her property. Andrew said that he had a feeling we would do well there and might even kill a brace; Valentine had a feeling that many prospective subscribers would come to the meet and Kate thought that we would get on to an old fox and have the run of the season. I was determined that I should be a perfect first whipper-in, and Laurence decided that he would go to bed very late on Friday in the hope of getting dark rings under his eyes, which, he said, would make him look considerably older.

Mrs. Simmons' property, which is called Little Stud, is nearly six miles from Long Chill Farm, and we decided that, to allow enough time for mishaps on the road, we must leave not later than half-past five.

Andrew wouldn't let any of us plait our horses' manes. Kate and I both thought we should because it would be a lawn meet. But Andrew was firm. "Plaited manes for cub-hunting?" he said scornfully. "What would hunting people say?" In the end Kate and I grumbled so much that he said we could wear our black coats to make up for horses unplaited manes.

Jane Browne and Roger Wilcox and the Haywards hacked over with us. Neither Jane nor Roger said any more than yes or no to any of our remarks, and we very soon stopped trying to talk to them.

It was a warm, sultry morning and our horses were unusually quiet. At first the roads were empty, but, by the time we reached the Hettington road, there were several milk lorries about and a few early risers on their way to work.

Soon it began to drizzle and Kate and I regretted our vanity, and wished that we were wearing mackintoshes, instead of our still comparatively new black coats.

The Hettington road is a proper country road: it is very narrow in places and runs alongside Middleborough Park for several miles; opposite the park is Middleborough Common and beyond that there are beech words. Ten years ago Middleborough Park was still the seat of the Marquis of Barkley, but taxation gradually drove him to sell his estate, and now the house and parkland belong to a national orphanage and the farmland is divided between neighbouring farmers.

We had been riding along the park fence for some time, when hounds' head suddenly went up, and Andrew said: "Ware deer."

Daystar's head had gone up too, and I could hear one of the horses behind snorting. I shouted "Hold up," to Charmer and Chastity, who were trying to slip past me without being seen, and dropped my thong. Hounds were all looking towards the common.

"There may be one out," said Andrew, by way of explanation. Kate was riding outside the pack, between them and the common. Valentine and Laurence had stopped talking. I felt rather useless in the front; if hounds broke away they would obviously break to the left across the common and then what was I to do? Ride on or stop and try to turn them back into the road? I had no time in which to decide for, at that moment, Tempest gave tongue, and within a second hounds were racing across the common in full cry. Fortunately, Valentine, Kate and Laurence were ready and they managed to head them before they reached the beech woods. Andrew blew a series of discords on his horn and, in about three minutes, we had two-thirds of the pack on the road again. Andrew rated them. Then we left Kate behind to bring on the rest, and continued in the direction of Hettington.

But our troubles were by no means over. We had only ridden a little way, when the hounds still on the common started to give tongue. The next moment Gladstone and Tell Tale slipped past me and, before I could turn Daystar round, had disappeared into a patch of gorse. Andrew said a word Laurence and I are not allowed to use, and then a whole herd of deer got up just in front of us and in a moment the whole pack had gone.

"Now we've had it," said Andrew in despairing accents. "It'll be hours before we get them all back."

I started to gallop across the common. "Try to stop them up against a fence, if you can," yelled Andrew.

"This'll make us hours late for the meet," said Laurence, suddenly beside me. "Of course, it would happen to-day just because there's a do."

Hounds had split. They were all hunting different deer, and as soon as we stopped them on one they started to hunt another. Andrew stood on the road and blew and blew. Valentine, Kate, Laurence and I grew hotter and hotter, and more and more disheartened. It wasn't long before we were split too. Soon I was deep in the beech woods trying to stop Charmer, True Love, Gladsome and Tell Tale hunting two does. I had only been in the woods once or twice before. I had no idea where I was heading for and very soon I was completely lost. Charmer, Gladsome, Tell Tale and True Love were enjoying themselves. They were hunting by sight and throwing their tongues like mad. The whole world seemed to echo with their cry. Daystar was excited too. She charged through immense brambles and acres of bracken pitted with rabbit holes. She nearly scraped me off under branches and recklessly plunged into bogs and over roots and tree stumps. Then hounds ran under a barbed-wire fence, across a ploughed field and into another wood. Daystar tried to jump the fence, but I stopped her in time. I wished I had wire cutters, but as I hadn't there was nothing I could do, except ride round the wood in search of a gate or a gap.

It was still raining. I looked at my watch and saw that it was half-past six. I expect you can imagine my feelings. I often wish I was one of those calm, phlegmatic people who don't worry whether they are late or early. Who say calmly, "Well, it's no good crying over spilt milk, or "What will be, will be," and quietly and sensibly settle down to the job in hand. Unfortunately, I'm not like that and, on this occasion, I became quite frantic. I charged backwards and forwards through that beastly wood, scratching my face, hitting my head on trees and riding poor Daystar into holes, roots, bogs and the most frightful brambles. All the time I could see Mrs. Simmons in my mind's eye waiting for us in front of her imitation Tudor farmhouse.

At last, I came to a place in the fence where the posts had fallen down and, jumping off Daystar, I stood on the wire and persuaded her to step over. Once on again I gave her head and we galloped full speed to where I had last heard hounds. Unfortunately, I could hear them no longer. There was no sound now but the depressing sound of falling rain. I turned Daystar and rode into the wood where I had seen hounds vanish.

There seemed no point in galloping any more. I wondered whether the others had been more successful. Perhaps they had collected the rest of the pack and were now at Little Stud, I thought optimistically, beginning to feel more cheerful.

The wood I was riding through was much nicer than the one I had just left. It had very little undergrowth and there were wide tracks and no visible stumps or roots to fall over. It was now seven o'clock and the rain was just beginning to come through my breeches. I wondered what I had better do; if I didn't find hounds, if nine o'clock came and I was still riding through unknown country should I try to find Little Stud or return to Long Chill Farm? I couldn't decide and then, suddenly, I thought I heard a whimper. I halted Daystar and listened. The rain was still falling; otherwie the wood seemed empty of sound. I rode on with a sinking heart and then I heard something which made my hopes soar. I heard the horn. It sounded very faint, and far, far away; but it cheered me and I trotted on through the wood feeling quite merry. Perhaps, I shall suddenly find myself on Mrs. Simmons' property, I thought hopefully. I might even bump into hounds in full cry. But, though I strained my ears, I didn't hear the horn again and soon I decided that what I had heard—both the whimper and the horn—had merely been the work of my imagination.

When I rounded a bend and suddenly saw Charmer, Gladsome, Tell Tale and True Love standing where two tracks crossed and looking incredibly sheepish and undecided, I couldn't believe my eyes. Evidently, they had lost the deer and, because of the blood on Tell Tale and True Love's muzzles, I guessed that they had been hunting rabbits. I called to them and rode on through the wood and then, as though one stroke of luck wasn't enough, I heard the horn, loud and clear this time and quite near.

Gladsome, Tell Tale, True Love and Charmer raced on ahead and Daystar broke into a canter. I felt overwhelmed with relief and, giving Daystar her head, we galloped on through the wood. I heard the horn again and it sounded even nearer this time, and then I heard Andrew blowing "All on" and "Come forrard," and I knew that Gladsome, Charmer, Tell Tale and True Love had joined him. A few more minutes, and I had reached a road and there were Kate, Andrew and my brother and what looked like the whole pack.

"All on," yelled Kate. "We've got them all. We've had such an awful time."

Andrew was riding on down the road. "Thank goodness you managed to stop them," he said.

I wanted to explain that they had stopped themselves, but no one seemed interested.

Kate would only say, "It's a quarter past eight," and Laurence, "This is going to be very bad for our reputation. We'll lose a great many prospective subscribers."

From their remarks I guessed that we were still heading for Little Stud, and that they like myself had spent the last two hours trying to stop hounds hunting deer. I noticed that Jane Browne, Valentine, Roger Wilcox and the Haywards were no longer with us.

"They went on to apologise to Mrs. Simmons," said Kate when I asked where they were. "I don't envy them. Dreadful though our job was, hanging about at

Little Stud waiting for us to turn up must be a hundred times worse."

"The dreadful thing is, we've lost Harry," she continued. "That's why Andrew's so het up. We all forgot all about him until about ten minutes ago, that's what's so dreadful. I only hope he's met the others or had the sense to ride to Little Stud."

"Do you think I should have gone to Mrs. Simmons, instead of Valentine?" asked Laurence, and I knew by his voice, that he felt guilty and had realised too late that the unpleasant task of apologising to Mrs. Simmons was the Master's job not the secretary's.

"I don't know," I answered. "I don't see that it really matters as long as someone does it."

"Oh, I wish we had never accepted the invitation," wailed Kate. "Everything's gone wrong. I'm sure we'll never find Harry, and Mum will be furious."

I wished that Valentine was with us. She can always calm Kate. Laurence said: "Wailing doesn't make it any better." I said: "Do shut up. I expect Harry's drinking cherry brandy with Mrs. Simmons." But our remarks had no effect on Kate; she continued to wail, frightening herself and us more each moment.

"He's probably broken his ankle," she said, "or fallen off and lost Lollipop, or worse still——" A whole string of horrible mishaps followed. Then she returned to Mrs. Simmons. "I bet she's furious," she said. "And all the local landowners, I bet they're fuming."

"Well, here we are at last," said Andrew, turning up a drive. "Don't let hounds pinch the eats. They've done enough to our reputation for one day."

Laurence straightened his hat. "Oh, look, there's

Lollipop!" shrieked Kate. "Oh, I am pleased. That must mean Harry's all right."

"Ssh," said Laurence. "Do try to be slightly more dignified."

A crowd came out of the house to meet us. Mrs. Simmons seized Laurence by the hand. "Don't mention it. Please don't mention it," she said, before he had time to speak. "We all understand just how you feel. But don't let it worry you. It doesn't matter the teeniest weeniest bit. This hour suits us better, really. Makes it seem so much longer, don't you know. It would have been so soon over otherwise. Now we've all been able to have a lovely cosy chat."

Then she left Laurence for Andrew and said exactly the same to him. Meanwhile, Laurence was taken indoors and Kate and I were given a glass of cherry brandy each, and large quantities of sausage rolls and oyster patties.

We didn't stay long at the meet. Very soon we were riding towards the first covert—a copse at the back of the house.

Mrs. Simmons led the way. She talked incessantly. She was riding a chestnut blood-mare of about fifteen hands called Sweety and, when she wasn't talking to one of us, she was talking to Sweety.

It had stopped raining but there were still low, heavy clouds in the sky. Kate and I each rode round one side of the copse. Andrew put hounds in and they found almost immediately. I had just halted Daystar when I saw a fox come out and slip away across the fields towards a distant spinney.

I blew my whistle and at the same moment hounds

broke into full cry. A few more seconds, and they were out of the copse and racing towards the spinney. Andrew was blowing the "gone-away." I galloped after hounds, thinking how insignificant our earlier troubles seemed now that hounds were running.

"This is almost too good to be true," called Andrew, who was just behind me.

Hounds had checked in the spinney. I dismounted and opened a gate. "Was he an old fox?" asked Andrew, riding through.

"Yes, I think so," I replied doubtfully. "He was quite big, anyway." I left the gate open for the field and followed Andrew and, in a few minutes, hounds were in full cry again. They crossed acres of stubble, then hunted into another spinney and they checked again.

"You go to the far end," Andrew told me. "Then you'll see him if he breaks."

Andrew jumped into the spinney over a stake-and-bound hedge. I galloped along the outside, but before I had reached the end, Andrew was blowing "gone to ground." I rode back and found Kate holding Mulligatawny. The field had dismounted. Mr. Watson, who had appeared as usual as if by magic, and Andrew were encouraging hounds to investigate the earth, and crying "Whoo' whoop wind 'im." I dismounted and loosened Daystar's girths.

"Oh, well, he was an old fox, anyway," said Andrew, taking Mulligatawny from Kate. "Next time we come round here we'd better try and stop the earths or they'll all be going to ground."

Everyone stood and talked for a few minutes. There

was quite a large field. Jane Browne and Roger Wilcox and the Haywards had joined us again. There were three or four children on leading reins and one on a Shetland pony, two on moorland ponies and several adults. The sky was clearing fast. Kate and I collected hounds together and we rode on to Mrs. Simmons' osier beds, where we found plenty of cubs.

I stood by the river banging my saddle flaps with my whip, but, in spite of my efforts and Kate's, the cubs ran from one osier bed to another and back again, and as soon as hounds settled on one, another appeared just in front of them. At half-past ten Andrew decided to call it a day. We said good-night to the field and thanked Mrs. Simmons for the meet and apologised once again for arriving so late. Mrs. Simmons said that it had been wonderful having us, that we must try and do it again soon, and that would we please forget all about the troubles of the morning? Because it would make her very unhappy to think of us worrying.

Soon we had left Little Stud far behind, but we still had Jane and Roger and the Haywards with us, so we still couldn't talk freely of the day's events. I wanted to know where the others were, while I rode round and round that first beastly wood looking for a gap in the wire fence. I wanted to know what Mrs. Simmons had said to Valentine when she appeared alone at the meet, and why Harry had vanished and whether Kate and Laurence had lost Andrew too, when we were trying to stop hounds hunting deer.

But it wasn't until hounds were fed and we were eating cake in the Days' kitchen that we could really discuss the events of the morning.

Valentine said that it had been awful arriving at the meet alone. Lots of people had already arrived and they were standing about asking where hounds were. Some of them were even preparing to go home, and Mrs. Simmons was in a terrible state. Apparently she had boasted about us to all the local people and they were just beginning to grow sarcastic when Valentine arrived.

"I felt smaller each moment," said Valentine. "And, oh, didn't time pass slowly? I thought you were never going to arrive. Fortunately, Mrs. Simmons didn't allow me much time for thinking; she talked and talked. I thought she would never stop. Then Harry turned up and we hoped he had good news, but of course he hadn't."

"It wasn't my fault," said Harry. "If Kate and Andrew will go jumping over four-foot stiles what do they expect me to do?"

"You don't know what a fright we had when we found you were missing," Kate told him.

"Don't let's talk about to-day any more," said Andrew, suddenly sounding just like Kate. "This is the second time we've looked fools in little more than a month. We've got to do better or we'll be the laughing stock of Flosshire, and that won't do us any good."

"Nor our bank balance," said Laurence. "We've got to pay Mr. Day the money we owe him before November the first and that's definite."

"Money, money, money; your brother always gets there in the end, Sandy," said Kate.

I washed and dried the mug out of which I had been drinking tea.

"Well, we had much better face facts," said Laurence firmly.

"Not to-day," said Andrew. "We've faced enough unpleasant facts already without getting on to money."

But, though the Days didn't have to face facts about money I had to — Laurence talked nothing else the whole way home. He said that we would be bankrupt by the end of the coming season if we didn't increase our subscribers by fifty per cent and cut down expenditure by a third. During the afternoon he worked it out on paper, so that he could prove his point to Valentine and Andrew next morning.

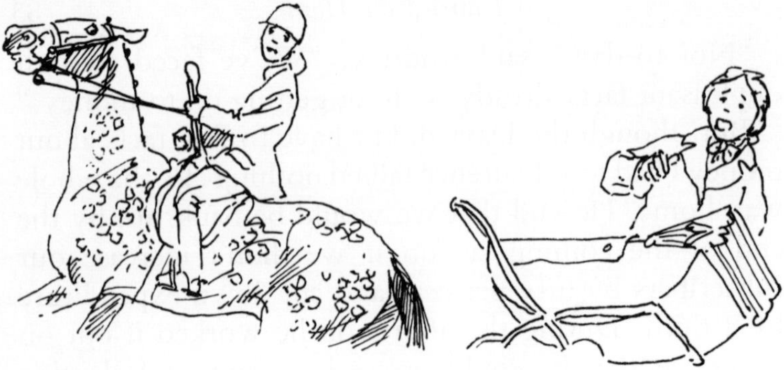

FIVE

October came warm and wet. Laurence continued to talk about money, and we agreed to raise our subscriptions. Our caps had to go up in comparison.

Valentine, Kate, Harry and I were back at school, and to me it was even worse than usual, now that Laurence was at home exercising horses and helping in the kennels, while I had to struggle with lessons in cold class-rooms, play hockey and do gym, with my thoughts miles away in the hunting field and with Laurence hacking Daystar through a countryside mellow with autumn.

We cub-hunted several times in October, but we didn't kill again and, though we enjoyed ourselves pottering about, we didn't really show much sport. It was because of that and because we had been late at Little Stud and had put up such a bad display on Bank Holiday, that we were determined we should show good sport on the day of the Opening Meet.

Colonel Hayward had invited us to Melcham for the Opening Meet and, on the Sunday before, we went there to look at the coverts. We were fairly familiar with Melcham having met there before; we knew the dangers of the railway line and the nearness of the main road. Colonel Hayward was more anxious to show us his neighbour's property than his own, and he very soon took us to Little Bottom Farm and introduced us to Mr. and Mrs. Brooks, who had only recently arrived in the district.

Mr. and Mrs. Brooks were comparatively young with three children of nine, twelve and fourteen and four point-to-point horses. They had already built several point-to-point fences on their farm, which they said we were welcome to practise over at any time, or jump out hunting. They were very glad to hear that we were meeting at Melcham on Saturday and said they they would be there, and that we could certainly draw their two coverts—Lot's Wood and Withy Copse.

Colonel Hayward then took us to see a Mr. Tegg who owned a dairy farm adjoining the Brooks' land. Mr. Tegg was a very old man with a beard. His wife had died years ago and now he had a housekeeper to look after him. We saw him in a room full of photographs of meets and horses, with antimacassars on the chairs, and the curtains half-drawn. He told us hunting anecdotes and about the horses he had owned and the hounds he had walked. He promised to come to the meet at Melcham and said that we could go where we liked on his land, and that he would tell his foreman to shut up the cattle and leave the gates open for us.

Later we had tea with the Haywards and Colonel Hayward told us that we should have a dinner for the farmers, and a point-to-point in the spring.

Driving home, we discussed the afternoon. We agreed that the Brooks were a useful addition to our country and that it would be fun jumping the point-to-point fences, though they looked rather enormous. Kate thought Andrew would be just like Mr. Tegg when he was old, and Andrew said he would never last so long. Then Laurence said: "But to be serious for a moment, what do you think of Colonel Hayward's suggestions? Why should we have a farmers' dinner? I can see the idea of having a point-to-point—you make money out of them. But why a dinner?"

Kate winked at me, and muttered: "Back to money. Oh, how I hate the word." Andrew said: "To get to know the farmers over whose land you hunt, of course. After all, they're pretty decent. They don't complain if we smash their fences, or cut their wire, or spoil their crops. I think a dinner would be rather fun."

"But who pays for it?" asked Laurence.

"Mostly us, I suspect," replied Andrew. "We ask people like Colonel Hayward and Mr. Austin-Smith, and they subscribe towards the cost. We foot the rest. But there's no need for it to be very much."

"I think it's a smashing idea," said Kate, sounding excited. "Where do we have it? In a private house or in an enormous hotel?"

"Generally in an hotel, I think," answered Andrew. "But quite honestly, I don't know much about farmers' dinners. I think Dad will know more. I remember he went to the Path Hill one once, anyway, and fell upstairs at three o'clock in the morning. Mum wasn't at all pleased."

"Oh, I think it'll be fun," cried Kate. "We'll be able

to have Mr. Smythe and Mr. Tegg, and lots and lots of other people."

"I think if we're going to have it we must do it properly," said Valentine.

"Well, we needn't decide about it yet," said Andrew. "We needn't have it till January or even later if we like."

"What about the point-to-point?" asked Laurence.

"Well, we can't do anything like that till March now," said Andrew. "Anyway, I don't think we can have one until we're recognised and that won't happen this season. What I do suggest is Hunter Trials. We wouldn't have to bother with *Weatherbys* then, nor give such large prizes and we could probably rake in several pounds from the car park."

"Sounds wonderful," I said. "Why didn't we think of it before?"

"What happens if it's wet?" asked Laurence.

"They come just the same," said Andrew, "and sit in their cars."

"Poor devils," said Laurence.

We turned down the lane to Long Chill Farm. "I had better write to the Masters' Association and try to get us recognised, hadn't I?" asked Valentine. "Otherwise, people like the Brooks won't want to bring their point-to-point horses out with us."

"Yes, I think you had," said Andrew. "Don't you think so, Laurence?"

"Definitely," Laurence agreed. "And I think we should hold some Hunter Trials in the spring, whatever happens. If we could only make five hundred pounds every year out of that kind of thing, we would be financially sound."

"We'll have to hold a ball," said Kate. "A wonderful Hunt Ball with champagne and oysters, and smoked salmon and meringues with real cream inside."

"And twenty pound tickets," said Valentine.

"Here we are," said Andrew. "I think we'll leave that for another season. We haven't got enough capital yet to gamble with balls and champagne. The band would probably cost two hundred pounds for a start."

We discussed the Farmers' Dinner several times during the following week, but without reaching any decision. Then Friday evening arrived, and we forgot everything but the morrow and all that was at stake. Laurence and I had tea at Long Chill Farm and, after tea, when the Days had cleaned their hunting kit you couldn't see the kitchen for clothes. Kate had spent most of the evening washing and her clothes were hanging on every conceivable hot pipe and on the Aga; at intervals they fell on the floor and then with many moans they had to be washed again. Harry used one of the best tea towels for polishing his boots, which caused a commotion, and then he upset the boot polish over Kate's white hunting-shirt, which she had just washed for the third time. Valentine calmed Kate and washed the tea-towel and the boot-blacked shirt. Harry burst into tears and Andrew sent him to bed. After that peace descended until Mrs. Day appeared. She was not pleased with the state of the kitchen; she told her children to take their boots upstairs and said that they would all get pneumonia through wearing damp clothes, and why, when they had weeks and weeks to get their clothes ready, did they always leave it to the last possible moment?

Valentine apologised. Laurence and Andrew carried all the boots upstairs, and Kate said: "Because we're half-baked imbeciles." Then she fetched the record player and a whole heap of records and Laurence, who had returned, and who doesn't appreciate Kate's taste in music, looked at his watch, and said: "We'll soon have to be going home."

Andrew said: "I'm sure tomorrow's going to be a flop. I feel it in my bones. I only hope I'm wrong again. Do you remember how silly we were the evening before the meet at Little Stud? How we were all so certain we were going to have a wonderful day and get lots of new subscribers?"

"If tomorrow's a flop, we've had it," said Laurence.

"Had it?" repeated Andrew.

"Yes, financially," said Laurence.

"Tomorrow we'll draw all the coverts blank," said Andrew. "There'll be hundreds of grumbling people, and, at the meet, someone will make a speech about teenagers. Later, Kate will run away across Colonel Hayward's special experimental crops and Laurence will fall off in front of the field. Valentine will lose the enormous cap she will have painstakingly collected and Sandy will kick our newest and richest subscriber's best horse. The field will ride over the terriers, ignore all Laurence's orders and lark over the Brooks' point-to-point fences, smashing most of them. I shall drop the horn into a pond right at the beginning of the day and hounds will hunt rabbits, ducks, deer and hares, but when someone halloas a fox away they just won't be interested."

Andrew paused for breath.

"And then it'll snow," continued Kate. "Like it did last season on that awful day we spent in the osiers by the river."

"Hounds will eat all the eats at the meet, like they did last season," I said. "And Mr. Watson will notice that all our girths are loose, and that both my garters are on the wrong way round, and that Kate's spurs are on upside down and goodness knows what else."

"Members of the field will be saying, 'Doesn't make enough noise, does he?' about Andrew, and, 'Are those really the whips?' and, 'Are those really all the hounds they've got?' all around us all day," said Laurence.

"It'll be dark by the time we start to ride home," I said, "and we'll have lost Tomboy and Tempest; and Pick and Shovel will have disappeared down an earth and——"

"But the field rode over them hours ago," interrupted Andrew.

"They're dead," said Kate.

"And then Dusty will kick Daystar," I continued.

"And we'll suddenly discover that we've lost Harry," said Kate, beginning to giggle.

"And Valentine, because she'll still be searching for the caps she lost earlier," said Andrew. "And all evening after we've got home there'll be angry telephone calls."

"We'll have dreadful dreams all night and next morning we'll all wake up with that awful sinking feeling you get after you've been a flop," said Kate.

"I think you had better give up the hunt," said Mrs. Day, whom we had forgotten was still in the kitchen, "if it's going to worry you so much. There's no point in making a toil out of a pleasure." (At last I knew from where Kate had collected that phrase.)

The Days all looked sheepish. None of them said anything.

"Come on, Sandy, we've still got the horses to feed," said Laurence. "It's after nine now."

"But you can't possibly go yet", cried Kate. "You haven't heard one record, and I fetched the record player especially for your benefit."

Laurence made a face at me. Kate put on a Beatles record.

When the record was played, Laurence and I borrowed Stubborn and Obstinate, two old bicycles, which Mr. Day had bought for ten pounds at a sale during the summer. We said good-bye to the Days and agreed to be at the kennels by nine in the morning. Then we started for home.

Stubborn and Obstinate had no lights and there was no moon to show us the way. I fell off three times and ran into Laurence twice and Laurence fell off once and ran into me five times. Then Obstinate's chain fell off and one of Stubborn's tyres burst with a loud report. By then I had a bruised elbow and a grazed hand, and Laurence had a chipped ankle and a bruised nose, and we were no longer on speaking terms with one another. We pushed and carried Obstinate and Stubborn into the garage in angry silence, and then we gave the horses the last feeds they have on the night before hunting because they always know when it's a hunting morning, and never eat their breakfast. Then we ate our supper and retired to bed still angry with one another.

cried: "Oh, isn't it wonderful to think that they're all ours? All nine couple. I'm sure we're going to have a lovely day today."

We all panicked then, and Andrew cried: "Touch wood." Valentine said: "Oh, Kate, how could you?" I said: "You've done it now."

When we had all touched wood we felt better, but we couldn't disguise our feelings any more. We whistled and sang and yelled remarks to each other about the Farmers' Dinner, and about becoming recognised and raising our subscriptions again.

Allate was greyer than ever beneath the grey sky. The tall trees were beautiful with a sheer, naked beauty and from the bakery came the tantalising smell of new bread. "Oh, I am hungry," cried Kate. "What wouldn't I give for a hunk of new bread and a piece of cheese?" I realised that Laurence and I had forgotten our sandwiches; that we hadn't even made them; the thought made me feel hungry too.

Melcham is four miles from Allate and when we were nearly there, Laurence said: "Do you know it's only ten o'clock?"

"No, not really?" cried Andrew, stopping Mulligatawny. "Why on earth didn't you tell me before?" Kate began to giggle.

Laurence said: "Well, you've got a watch, haven't you?"

"Of course I have," replied Andrew. "But I can't be looking at it every other moment." I wondered whether there was going to be a row. Andrew and Laurence were glaring at one another.

"Well, what do we do now?" demanded Andrew.

"Hoofs—I hear hoofs," shrieked Harry. "They're coming towards us."

"Oh, gosh, what are we going to do?" cried Kate, still giggling. "We can't possibly get to the meet nearly an hour early."

Three riders came round a bend in the road. They were wearing ratcatchers and hard hats.

"How much farther is it?" asked Laurence.

"About ten minutes' ride," answered Andrew. "I bet these people stop and ask a lot of tiresome questions."

"Hold up, hold up together," I shouted as Tomboy and Rattler started to slip away together.

"Let them go," said Andrew. "It'll give us an excuse for being here."

The three riders had reached us now. They were all adults and the eldest, a grey-haired woman, halted the weedy chestnut she was riding, and said: "Can we do anything to help? Are you in trouble?" Andrew raised his hat, and said: "That's all right, madam. A couple of hounds have just slipped away down to the farm, but we'll have them back in a moment." Then he glared furiously at Kate and me, but neither of us knew whether he wanted us to pursue Rattler and Tomboy or stay where we were, and believing in "when in doubt do nothing," stayed still. For an awful moment, I thought the three riders meant to wait with us until we had collected our missing couple of hounds. But after looking at us rather hard they rode on, and we all sighed with relief.

"Now, for goodness' sake, fetch Rattler and Tomboy back," said Andrew, "before they *do* get into mischief."

I started to ride away and so did Kate. "But don't

Saturday morning dawned warm and cloudy. The wind was in the south-west; and from the moment I wakened everything seemed set for success. I wakened to the first ring of my clock and I knew at once what day it was and what was to happen. I ran into Laurence in the passage; he must have been awake for some time, because he already had on his dressing-gown and bedroom slippers. Daystar and Overture were unusually clean and for once the grooming tools and plaiting implements were in the stable cupboard. The horses were far calmer than usual and Daystar actually ate some of her morning feed. By ten to eight, she and Overture were groomed, plaited, saddled and standing with their feet oiled. By half-past eight, we were dressed. We gave each other a last look over; Laurence noticed that one of my boot-tabs was visible, and I noticed that one of Laurence's garters was between the second and third button on his breeches, instead of the first and second. I pushed the offending tab into my boot with a fork, and Laurence altered his offending garter, then we shouted good-bye to our parents, bridled our hunters, and rode down into the valley.

There was no sign of the Days when we arrived at Long Chill Farm; but our watches told us that it was only five to nine, so we didn't worry.

Soon we heard a window flung open and, looking towards the house, we saw Mrs. Day. "They're just coming," she called. "One of the buttons on Kate's shirt fell off, and Harry lost his tie-pin."

"It's all right, we're early," I called back.

"That's typical of Kate and Harry," said Laurence. At that moment the Days arrived in a rush.

"It's only just nine," cried Kate.

"You were early," said Valentine.

"We're in tons of time," said Andrew. "It's not much more than an hour's hack."

"Can't see why you want to start so early," said Mr. Day, appearing from the cowshed. "You'll be there by ten o'clock."

"We're allowing for accidents," replied Kate. "We don't want to be late again. It was too frightful last time."

Andrew was letting hounds out.

"See you at the meet then," said Mr. Day. "I'd better go and get a wash now and have a bit of breakfast."

Valentine was leading Mulligatawny out of the stable. Hounds followed Mr. Day towards the kitchen door. I turned them back.

"Grand morning for scent," said Andrew, mounting Mulligatawny. "They ought to run all right to-day."

We all felt very cheerful as we rode out of the valley towards Allate. The horses were fresh, but not too fresh, and, except for finding a carcase, fighting over it, and upsetting the Days' dustbin, hounds were behaving beautifully.

I think we all felt proud of our pack; hounds looked so fit and their eyes were shining and, though they were longing to break away and draw the neighbouring woods, they stayed together behind me and in front of Kate. But, though we all felt optimistic, none of us dared to voice our feelings. We were too frightened of "pride comes before a fall," and of a repetition of all which happened before the meet at Little Stud. Kate did throw caution to the winds once. She suddenly both go," cried Andrew in exasperated accents. "I want someone to keep the rest of the pack together."

"I'll go, it's my job," said Kate, meaning that she was second whipper-in.

"What's the time?" asked Andrew.

"Can't he look at his own watch?" muttered Laurence.

"Ten past ten," answered Valentine.

"Is that all?" said Andrew. We heard Kate crack her whip, and then we saw Rattler and Tomboy coming back across the field on our left.

"We can't possibly get there before twenty to eleven," said Andrew.

"Oh, dear, why did we have to start so early?" asked Valentine.

"To be on the safe side," said Laurence. "After to-day, I think we had better stick to the dangerous one. At least it's more amusing."

"There's a dead cow down by the farm in a pit," yelled Kate. "It smells awful. I bet hounds keep going there all day. You can smell it from a mile off."

"I can't," said Laurence.

"This is going to be a lovely day," said Andrew gloomily.

"Another moment and some more people on their way to the meet will appear," said Laurence.

"Why are you all so cross?" cried Kate. "I think it's jolly funny. It's much better to be early than late."

"'Ware Mr. Watson," shrieked Harry.

"Is he coming?" cried Kate in horrified accents.

"This is the last straw," said Andrew, sounding desperate.

"Let's go on!" I cried, thinking that anything would

be better than twenty minutes of Mr. Watson.

"Ssh," said Valentine. "He'll hear."

"We can't possibly get to the meet before twenty to eleven," said Andrew. "It would be sheer bad manners."

Mr. Watson was carrying his usual walking-stick and was dressed, as always, in breeches, long socks, ordinary boots and an old tweed hacking-jacket. "Good-morning," he called cheerfully. "What keeps you?"

"The hour," called Kate, who doesn't really mind Mr. Watson, though she always pretends she hates him.

"Pull up your girths everyone," said Andrew. "I can see half Flosshire between yours and Daystar," he told me.

"Check your boot-garters," said Laurence.

"And your spurs," added Valentine.

Mr. Watson had reached us by now. "Grand morning," he said cheerfully, with a laugh. "You should find a fox all right today. Do you expect many at the meet? The usual crowd, I suppose. Hounds look well; though old Vampire's a bit on the lean side. Hear you've put up your subscription; quite right too; time you did. If people want to hunt, they must pay for it. Too many people expect everything for nothing nowadays." While Mr. Watson talked he ran his eye over all of us.

Kate winked at me and began to giggle. I giggled too, and Valentine frowned at both of us.

"It's nice to see you all in black coats this season," continued Mr. Watson. "I expect they cost you a pretty penny, though. Did you go to London for them?"

Mr. Watson's curiosity is one of the most annoying things about him; where money's concerned it is almost unbearable.

"That's right," said Laurence.

"Still I expect your fathers are always ready to spill the cash, aren't they?" asked Mr. Watson.

"How many does he think we've got?" muttered Andrew.

"Mine was a present and I had it last season," said Valentine.

"Isn't it time we rode on?" asked Laurence. "We don't want to be late at the meet."

"I'll come along with you," said Mr. Watson. "Your ponies look well, I must say. Are they the same as you had last season?"

It was twenty to eleven when we turned up Melcham's drive. We could see a horse box parked under the trees by the house, and there was already a crowd of foot followers on the lawn.

"This is becoming an annual event for the village," said Laurence.

"Good thing, too; I believe in tradition," said Andrew.

The three riders who had passed us on the road were talking to Colonel Hayward by the steps in front of Melcham's white front door. Mrs. Hayward, in trousers and a silk blouse, was offering a tray of eats to some children on unclipped ponies.

"One of you had better stand by the ha-ha and the other by the front door," Andrew told Kate and me, as Wasteful made a dive in that direction, "And look out for Valiant," he added. "Remember what he was like last time."

Mrs. Hayward saw us and waved. Hounds dashed towards her, their eyes on the tray she carried.

"Hold up, hold up together," I shouted, and I cracked my whip and it actually made a noise—just as I had always hoped it would one day—a noise like a pistol shot. Hounds turned back. Andrew said: "I wish there was a corner where we could hold them up. It's so difficult to keep them together with lawns all around and flower-beds."

Mr. Watson laughed, and said: "I'll keep them off the lawn."

Kate thanked him, and I thought how helpful he was and how we would like him if he wasn't so curious.

Mrs. Hayward called: "Do come in, some of you. Everyone's inside."

"Go on," said Andrew to Valentine and Laurence.

"We always feel so awful leaving you and Kate and Sandy outside, don't we, Valentine?" said Laurence.

"Don't be silly, you get the worst of it in lots of ways. Anyway, I hate going in," said Andrew. "I haven't any parlour manners. I would much rather be out here with hounds."

"So would I," said Kate.

An old man offered to hold Golden Syrup and Overture, and Valentine and Laurence disappeared indoors.

"I hope they're not going to be hours," said Harry. "Once they start drinking they never stop."

"Ssh," said Andrew. "You make it sound as though they're drunkards. And, anyway, it's quite untrue. They never have more than one."

"Haven't you had anything to drink yet?" asked

Colonel Hayward, coming across. "I say, they haven't been looking after you very well, have they? What will you have? There's cherry brandy, sherry——"

"We'd all like cherry brandy, please, I think, sir, thank you very much," said Andrew, looking at Kate and me.

"And lemonade for Harry," suggested Colonel Hayward.

"That would be lovely, thank you very much," said Andrew, not daring to look at Harry.

"It *is* unfair," complained Harry, when Colonel Hayward had vanished indoors. "When shall I be old enough for cherry brandy?"

"Ssh," said Andrew.

Mrs. Hayward was approaching with a tray loaded with oyster-patties, sausage-rolls, slices of bacon, egg flan and cheese-straws. "Take your pick," she said.

Kate and I found it difficult to stop hounds grabbing the eats. Andrew helped himself to an oyster-patty and a sausage-roll and, when Mrs. Hayward had gone, he fed the sausage to hounds which kept them together. I took two cheese-straws and Kate had a slice of ham and egg flan. Harry had already been given an iced cake with his lemonade.

All the time more people were arriving: the local riding school turned up in full force, with ten children on ponies and two adults to look after them. Jane Browne and Roger Wilcox arrived together. Many more foot followers appeared, and smart horses were led out of the horse box under the trees.

"We should collect some caps today," said Andrew.

Mr. Austin-Smith arrived complete with trailer.

Hounds were becoming restless. I wished that Valentine and Laurence would appear. But, since it was only just eleven, I knew we wouldn't see them for at least another ten minutes. Mr. Austin-Smith had a word with Andrew; then he disappeared indoors. Harry sighed. Valiant had his eye on the front door. Twice I stopped him on the steps. Wasteful and Tomboy were more interested in the back of the house. Tempest, Spendthrift and Tell Tale wanted to explore the ha-ha. Kate, Mr. Watson and I were soon rushing backwards and forwards all the time, and the crowd on the lawn seemed always in the way. Kate hit a tall woman wearing spectacles with her whip, and I upset a pram. The tall woman complained bitterly and, though the baby inside the pram wasn't hurt, its mother was far from pleased. Andrew was completely nerve-racked by these mishaps and, whenever Kate or I moved, he said: "Mind the prams," and "Don't hit anyone", and "Mind the turf and don't ride over the borders."

All three of us were relieved when, at last, Valentine, Colonel Hayward and Laurence appeared. Harry said: "Hurray," and Kate said: "I thought they were never going to return." Mr. Austin-Smith unboxed his seventeen-hand grey hunter and everybody started to mount. One of the riding school ponies ran backwards and kicked Jane Browne's pony on the knee. Valentine and Laurence were grinning. They came across to us and Valentine delved into her pockets and said: "I thought perhaps you wouldn't get offered these," and handed us each a chicken sandwich.

Laurence said: "There was a dickens of a crowd inside. The Brookses were there. They've just gone back to Little Bottom Farm to fetch their horses. They're meeting us at the first covert."

Kate, Andrew and I thanked Valentine for the sandwiches.

"They'll have to hurry," said Andrew, alluding to Mr. and Mrs. Brooks, I suppose. Felicity and Patience appeared riding their ponies, Joker and Jester.

"Shall we show you the way?" asked Patience. "It's the same covert as we drew last year; but this time we've stopped all the neighbouring earths."

"That's grand," said Andrew. Laurence thanked Colonel and Mrs. Hayward for the meet. Someone took some photographs. I was scowling and Kate told me afterwards that she had her mouth open. Then someone said: "Hounds, please," and I led the way down the drive on a prancing, dancing Daystar.

SIX

When we were half-way across the park, Andrew sent me on ahead to stand by the oak tree in the ploughed field by the railway line.

I had been previously instructed to head foxes away from the line and to be ready to stop goods trains, but to stop hounds if they ran that way, rather than expresses. Kate was sent to the main road with instructions to hold up the traffic if hounds ran in her direction.

I felt very excited but rather overcome by so much responsibility, standing by the oak tree, while Andrew put hounds into the plantation fifty yards or more away. Daystar was impatient. She thought I was very silly standing so far away from everyone else. She dug and snatched at her bit and banged me on my nose with her head. I knew that a fox might appear at any moment. I kept my eye glued to the plough between me and the plantation. The field were standing near where Andrew had put hounds in; I could hear them talking. I nearly blew my whistle when a hare came out and disappeared across the plough. An express roared along the line. Not far ahead was the hedge I had jumped last season on the day of the opening meet. I hoped hounds would run that way today. I hoped that they would run for miles and miles, and so dispel Andrew's gloom and lift Laurence above his endless money worries. Daystar continued to dig. I started to count the ridges of plough. Andrew blew a few notes on the horn. The field were still talking: I couldn't distinguish words, but I could hear a steady hum of voices. Tomboy and Wishful came out on to the plough. For a moment Tomboy spoke, and I had appalling visions of a fox I hadn't seen. I braced myself to stop goods trains. Then he and Wishful returned to the plantation. The landscape stretched bare and brown and shabby green to the main Chidlington road. Andrew blew hounds out and, turning Daystar, I galloped to the far side of the plantation, where I met him and Kate, and Laurence and the field.

"We're going to draw the firs next," Andrew told me.

The firs were dark and mysterious. According to a notice on a gate, they had once won a prize for the best firs in Flosshire.

Hounds found almost immediately. I was marking the top right-hand corner. Kate was on the left side, and soon I heard her whistle, clear and urgent.

I galloped round the firs and reached the far side just as hounds were breaking. Andrew was blowing the "gone-away" and cheering them on. Kate was galloping on ahead hoping to view the fox as he left a copse we could see in the distance.

Hounds were throwing their tongues beautifully.

The whole countryside seemed to ring with their cry. They were running very fast and, except for Spendthrift who was nowhere to be seen, all together.

Andrew and I galloped on side by side. Soon hounds checked and then hunted slowly through a herd of cattle.

"Slip on ahead and open the gate," said Andrew, pointing to a five-barred gate set in a wire fence. I sent Daystar on.

The gate was stiff and I had only just managed to open it when Andrew arrived. "Get up, get up," he shouted, galloping through. "The field are just behind; they'll shut it."

Daystar stood beautifully while I mounted. Hounds were in full cry again. I gave Daystar her head and caught up with Andrew. "This is wonderful," he said. "Look at the way the young hounds are hunting. Look at Tell Tale and True Love."

We reached the copse and there was Kate on the other side, blowing her whistle and holding up her hat.

"He's only about two minutes ahead," she shouted, sounding excited. In the distance we could see Ashbury Wood.

"I bet he goes there," said Andrew.

For a moment we galloped on abreast. The field was close behind. In front was plough and another wire fence. Down in one corner we could see some rails, and we turned towards them with one accord. There was a ditch in front of the rails and above were the branches of a nearby tree.

"Nasty place," muttered Andrew, taking it slowly on Mulligatawny. I was glad I wasn't riding a seventeen-hand hunter as I rode Daystar at the rails. She jumped neatly and the next moment Dusty was over too, and we were all galloping on towards Ashbury Wood.

Hounds were hunting more slowly across the plough. Our gallop became a canter. "Shall I go on ahead and see if he slips into Ashbury Wood?" asked Kate.

"That'll be grand," answered Andrew.

"What about me?" I asked.

"You stay here with me," said Andrew. The field were still close behind. We could hear Felicity and Patience praising their ponies. Mr. and Mrs. Brooks had taken their own line and now they were slightly ahead of hounds on the plough, which didn't please Andrew. Mr. Austin-Smith's hunter was blowing a good deal and I decided he must be going in the wind.

Hounds hunted into a few acres of kale. I galloped on to mark the far corner, but before I reached it, they were out on the plough again and running like smoke towards Ashbury Wood. Andrew and I jumped a low hedge, galloped across a field of grass and then we had reached some slip-rails and a track into Ashbury Wood.

I took down the rails, which had wire along the top, and, leaving them for the field to put up again, followed Andrew.

Ashbury Wood is five hundred acres or more in size. It lies between Chidlington and a small village called Letchbury near where it joins Withy Common, which consists mostly of gorse and bracken, and covers about a hundred acres.

Kate had already disappeared. Hounds were crashing about in the undergrowth. They sounded very fierce and were making a tremendous noise.

"If you slip on to the far end, you might see a fox come out," Andrew told me.

"Okay," I said, thinking that I wouldn't need to be told if I was a competent whipper-in, and galloping on down the track.

It was ages before I saw light shining through the trees and reached the end of the track, and knew that soon I would be out of the wood. Daystar was sweating and I couldn't hear hounds any more. I rode out of the wood into a partly ploughed field. I scanned the unfamiliar landscape for a fox and saw in the distance only a tractor moving slowly. Should I wait a moment longer, I wondered, or go back and risk the fox coming out without my seeing him? I dithered. I rode into the wood and out again. I strained my ears and tried to make Daystar stand still, while I listened. Then I decided to ride back.

Ashbury Wood seemed very quiet now. Rabbits and squirrels scurried across the track and once a pheasant flew up just in front of us. But there was no sign of hounds. I had an awful sinking feeling. I thought of the run I was missing and that instead of becoming a better and more efficient whipper-in, I was growing worse each week.

Daystar was frantic: she hates losing hounds even for a moment and now she was quite oblivious of ruts and holes and patches of bog and fallen branches as we galloped back along the track. We reached the rails where we had first entered Ashbury Wood and, except for hoof-marks, there was nothing to show that hounds had ever passed that way. They seemed to have vanished into thin air. My sinking feeling grew worse. I felt near despair. I knew that I had lost hounds and I had no idea in which direction to go. Daystar was snatching and pulling; she was certain hounds had run towards Withy Common. I looked at the ground and saw hoof-prints leading in that direction, and let her have her own way. Very soon the track to Withy Common petered out, and we were galloping through thick undergrowth and under a multitude of overhanging branches. But nothing seemed to daunt Daystar. She was determined to reach Withy Common as quickly as possible; and, though I had long ago lost track of the hoof-prints and hadn't heard the horn for ages, I was certain she must know where hounds were and be taking me to them.

At last, we reached the common and, after ploughing through acres of bracken, we came to the winding country road which takes you down into grey, rambling Letchbury. Daystar still knew where hounds had gone—they had turned right towards the village. But I believed her no longer. In the fields across the road, the cows were grazing peacefully. A dog was busy hunting rabbits by himself on the common. It was obvious that hounds had not been near Withy Common for some time, if at all.

I rode down into the village. It was lunch-time and there was no one about. Every moment I hoped to see someone come up the road on a bicycle. I was ready to stop a car, or lorry or bus, or anything which had a driver which might have seen hounds. But all Letchbury was enjoying its lunch-hour and, at last, in exasperation, I stopped at the village shop and, dismounting, opened the door. I had to shout "Good morning," and "Good afternoon", and "Hoi," before anyone appeared. Then the woman who came to the counter wiping her hands on her apron, turned out to be deaf. After we had talked at cross-purposes for some time, she disappeared in search of her son and I had visions of hounds hunting across our own valley and killing in our garden at home. The deaf woman's son said that he had not heard any hounds come through the village, but that he had been out with the van all morning, so that they might have come without knowing it. "Which hounds would they be?" he asked, preparing for a chat. I explained and apologised for bothering him and his mother, and then I mounted Daystar and rode back through Letchbury feeling more gloomy than ever.

I halted Daystar when I reached Withy Common and tried to decide what to do next. But my brain wasn't working very well and I could only think of my own incompetence—that I must be the worst whipper-in ever to have existed, that I had let down the hunt in its most critical hour—instead of deciding my next action.

Finally, I decided to ride back into Ashbury Wood and listen. It was just possible hounds might have been there all the time, I thought. They might have checked, and then if Andrew hadn't blown his horn how could I have heard them? I felt hope return. Daystar was willing to go anywhere. She tore across the common, plunging recklessly through the bracken and banging my legs against trees.

We were just entering Ashbury Wood when I thought I heard a whimper. I halted Daystar, and then I heard a yap and the next moment I saw Pick chasing rabbits through the undergrowth. I shouted: "Pick, Pick, hold up together, out of it." She stopped hunting rabbits; but, instead of coming towards me, she started to run away through Ashbury Wood. My heart sank. I saw myself pursuing Pick through Ashbury Wood on to Withy Common and back again while hours passed, and the afternoon became evening and the evening became night. I followed her, calling, and then I heard a sound which filled me with hope. I heard hoofs on the Letchbury road. Daystar had heard them too, and she swung round and listened. I had lost sight of Pick. I rode back through Ashbury Wood. I had visions of Andrew and Valentine and Kate and Laurence and the field all on the Letchbury road. I used my legs and Daystar's trot became a canter, and then suddenly I saw something grey coming towards me through the trees, and the next moment I saw Kate and Dusty, and Kate shouted "Hallo," and Daystar neighed.

I was filled with relief. I imagined, I can't think why, that Kate had been sent to find me and that now we would ride back to where everyone else was waiting for us. Kate's next words filled me with horror and then dismay. "But where's everyone else?" she shouted.

So she was lost too, I realised. Both the whippers-in were lost and it was the day of the opening meet. I felt too dreadful for words to describe. I saw Andrew hacking home without Kate or I to ride in front and behind. I imagined everyone's remarks at the end of the day when they took their separate ways for home and there were still no whippers-in to be seen. Kate had reached me now.

"Where's everyone else?" she repeated.

"I don't know," I said. "When did you lose sight of them?"

"When I left you and Andrew hours ago," answered Kate. "You know, before we even entered this beastly wood. You're lost, too, then. When did you lose them?"

"Just afterwards," I answered, watching Kate's face become still gloomier. "I was sent to the end of the wood and by the time I reached it, they had gone."

"But I was there. I told Andrew I was going to be there," said Kate. "Why on earth did he send you there?"

"I've no idea," I said. "And I don't really care. The point is, what are we going to do?"

"I can't see how we missed each other," said Kate. "I suppose you didn't come quite so far round. Where did you go when you found you were lost?"

I explained. Kate had turned away from Letchbury towards Chidlington when she had reached the road. That was how we had missed one another. "Why, here's Pick," said Kate. "Where did she turn up from?"

I explained how I had heard her yap and then how she had run away, and together we caught her. I mounted and Kate handed me Pick, before we rode on through Ashbury Wood to the trails where Andrew and I had entered hours and hours ago. We didn't talk much. We were both too gloomy. It had been bad enough being lost on our own, but to be lost together was infinitely worse. We had both imagined the other one whipping-in. Now the thought of the hunt without either whipper-in was almost unbearable.

Kate took down the rails and we rode through, and

she put them up again. In the distance we could see cows standing round a farmyard waiting to be milked.

"What are we going to say to Andrew? Oh, why are we so stupid?" wailed Kate, as we rode on across the plough over which we had galloped so cheerfully in the morning.

"It would happen today of all days," I said.

"What's the time?" asked Kate.

"Ten past two," I said, looking at my watch without much interest.

"Is that all?" cried Kate. "We might find them yet. I thought it was much later than that. Come on, let's gallop."

Galloping on an excited Daystar with Pick in my arms wasn't easy. My reins became steadily longer. I couldn't shorten them without letting go of Pick, and Daystar was completely out of control by the time we reached the wire fence between us and the firs. For an awful moment I thought Daystar meant to take the wire fence in her stride. Then she stopped with two sickening jolts.

After that Kate took Pick and we rode more quietly. Soon we reached the small hamlet beyond Melcham, and I asked a man digging in his garden whether he had seen hounds recently. He told us that they hadn't been near since the morning and, as we rode on again towards Allate, we felt gloomier than ever.

The time was now three o'clock. The day was growing steadily colder; the wind had veered to the east and the sky had turned a lighter grey.

"We might as well go home," said Kate, when we reached the cross-roads near Melcham. "We'll never find them now."

"But it'll be dreadful if we're already home when the others get back," I said. "It'll look as though we hardly bothered to search for them."

"I don't see why," answered Kate. "Anyway, we won't be home before four. And I bet they're packing up now, unless they're still running. It's too jolly cold for people to want to go on and on hunting."

I was persuaded, and so we took the road for home and the horses pulled and hurried, doubtless thinking of hot gruels and of deep beds of golden straw and of mixture hay.

I don't think I shall ever forget that ride home. Long before we reached Allate our hands and feet were numb with cold. The wind grew steadily more bitter. It seemed to penetrate into the very marrow of our bones. It rushed round corners in dreadful gusts, stinging our already cold faces. The horses continued to jog and pull. They were cold too, and soon we threw caution and principles to the winds and let them spank along the road at a fast trot. There were few people about. In many houses the curtains were already drawn. I was too cold to care any more about us having been lost. I only wanted to be at home in a hot bath and to know that downstairs in the dining-room a boiled egg and hot crumpets awaited me.

Our valley looked bleak and bare and empty when we turned off the Allate road and saw it there before us. We scanned the landscape hopefully, expecting to see hounds jogging along the lane to the kennels. But no such welcome sight greeted us. The valley seemed empty of life, and our hearts sank again.

"We've raced them," I said, and wondered what Bert Saunders and Mr. and Mrs. Day would say when we told them our story. But there was no one to greet us when at last we reached the kennels.

"They must be still at Chidlington Market," said Kate, referring to her parents. I held Pick while Kate put Dusty in her box; then I rode home across the valley.

Mr. Mitchell had put everything ready in Daystar's box, and in a very short time she was rugged and bandaged, and I raced indoors to warm my aching hands and feet. My parents hadn't heard Daystar's hoofs on the drive, but they rushed into the kitchen when they heard the back door open.

Mummy said: "How did the day go off?" Daddy said: "Did you kill a brace?" I said: "Awful and no." And Mummy said: "Come and get warm by the fire. You look perished. I've turned the boiler up, so you can have a bath straight away if you like."

I told my parents all about the day, while I took off my boots and warmed my hands. They were very sympathetic. Mummy said that it might have happened to anyone, and Daddy said that my getting lost wouldn't alter the fate of nations.

I wanted to go back to Long Chill Farm when I had finished telling my story, and to help feed hounds and settle the horses for the night, but my parents wouldn't hear of it. They said that the Days employed Bert Saunders to do that, and that, anyway, by the time I had walked to the kennels, everything would probably be done. So after a short argument I gave in and had my bath, and when I was in the middle of it I heard Laurence come home. I was very cowardly and stayed in my bath until my parents had told Laurence the gist of my story. But I needn't have worried, because Laurence was quite sympathetic, having been lost himself for a short while during the day.

We had tea together, and Laurence told me what had happened after I vanished along the track through Ashbury Wood. Apparently, the fox had swung right and started to run back towards the firs. But when he was half-way across the plough the Brookses had headed him and, turning right again, he had crossed the Letchbury road and run towards Chidlington.

"We were all beginning to wonder where you were by then," continued Laurence, "But we didn't worry. Hounds were hunting beautifully. I've never seen them hunt so well. We had been running for about forty minutes and then the fox ran through those allotments this side of Chidlington, and on through some suburban houses' gardens, and a lot of anti-blood sports people came out and shrieked at us, and then we lost him somewhere near the gas works. After that we didn't do much. We knew we had lost you and Kate, and we discovered that Spendthrift and Gladsome were missing too. We hung about for a bit and Valentine whipped-in, and Andrew blew and blew. We drew a messy little osier bed by the gas works until the owner appeared and threatened to summons us for trespass; and then people started to go home, and it seemed to get colder and colder, and at ten past three we decided to call it a day. We took a long time getting home, because we rode round by Melcham hoping to collect you and Kate and Spendthrift and Gladsome. But we didn't see any of you and we gradually got colder and colder, and Andrew and Valentine quarrelled over some wretched little argument they had weeks ago, and Harry snivelled because his hands were cold and altogether it was dreadfully dismal. And then we reached the kennels and Bert Saunders wasn't there, nobody knows why, and the coppers had gone out and Kate was in her bath, and everyone was very unpleasant. You know what the Days can be like when everything goes wrong."

I did and I could see it all. Andrew and Valentine passing each other with furious faces. Kate shrieking "Where were you?", from the bathroom. "Fortunately, I couldn't stop because of Overture getting cold," Laurence continued. "But I felt rather mean leaving them everything to do."

I felt horribly guilty. I wished that my parents hadn't persuaded me to stay at home. I imagined Andrew lighting the coppers with numb fingers and Valentine putting the horses to bed and then helping Andrew feed hounds and look them over for cuts and thorns. "I shall go and ring Andrew up now," I said.

"I shouldn't if I were you," said Laurence. "I should give him a few minutes' peace first. He's probably in his bath by now."

I hesitated. I wanted to make my apologies and tell my story as soon as possible. I didn't want them to hang over me all evening. Then the telephone bell rang. "I'll go," I said. I braced myself for one of the Days. A hundred possibilities flashed into my mind—a hound might be in a trap miles away. Pick might be having fits. The horses might be out. Perhaps we were to deal with an angry farmer, or the owner of the gas works, or some of the anti-blood sports people. Anything might have happened. I picked up the receiver, and said: "Hallo, Sandy here." I was amazed when rather a shrill voice answered. I wondered who it could be, and so missed the first words, and had to say: "I'm so sorry, I didn't hear. What did you say?"

The voice said: "It's Mrs. Woods speaking from twenty-four Buckingham Drive. Is that Mr. Dashwood's house?"

I said: "Yes, that's right," and was just about to call Daddy when Mrs. Woods said: "Will you tell him that one of his dogs is on my bed and won't get off. I rang up the police and they said I had better get in touch with you. He's been on there since one o'clock and he's spoiling the eiderdown, and has made the sheets and pillow-cases filthy with his dirty paws."

She paused for breath, and then I did something awful: I couldn't stop myself. The thought of Spendthrift or Gladsome curled up on someone's bed in Buckingham Drive was too funny—I giggled. Mrs. Woods sniffed, and said: "Who is that?" in a cross voice.

"Sandy Dashwood, first whip to the Chill Valley Foxhounds," I said, trying to make up for my ill-mannered giggle. "I am extremely sorry such an unfortunate situation has occurred. I will send the van immediately to collect the hound."

"I don't dare touch him," said Mrs. Woods. "I called to him and offered him cake, but he won't move, and when my husband gets home and sees him I don't know what he'll say. He raided the larder as soon as he arrived and had our Sunday joint."

I was feeling awful now. I decided Mrs. Woods was being jolly decent about the whole affair and I wished I hadn't giggled.

"I am terribly sorry," I said.

"Well, please come quickly," said Mrs. Woods. "Number twenty-four, Buckingham Drive is the address. It's part of the new estate south of the gas works and the name is Woods."

"Right," I said, trying to sound business-like. "We'll be with you inside half an hour."

I put down the receiver and thought of Spendthrift lying on an eiderdown.

"Who the dickens was that?" asked Laurence, when I returned to the dining-room. I explained, and Laurence said: "It's just one thing after another. I suppose it's Spendthrift again. He is a useless hound."

I said: "Shall I ring up the Days?"

Laurence said: "I suppose we'll have to," in weary accents.

Then Daddy, who was also in the dining-room, said: "Why shouldn't I run you to Buckingham Drive in the car?"

Laurence and I accepted Daddy's offer without hesitation and, while Laurence put on his hunting-boots again, I fetched my overcoat and dragged a comb through my hair.

We didn't ring up the Days; they generally have to deal with all the unpleasant telephone calls, and we were delighted to be able to settle a tiresome matter without them for once.

We found Buckingham Drive quite easily, and, after some time, number twenty-four, which was a semi-detached house, with gables and crazy-paving leading to the front door.

"I'll wait in the car," said Daddy. "Don't be too long."

"Did she sound very cross?" asked Laurence, as we approached the front door.

"Not too bad," I answered, deciding that she would have grey hair and be small with a long nose. We knocked and Mrs. Woods turned on the porch light and opened the front door. She was small with mouse-coloured hair. She was wearing a plain blue wool dress.

"He hasn't stirred since I rang you up," she said, leading the way upstairs. "I hope there's nothing wrong with him. I'm not used to dogs."

We followed Mrs. Woods into a bedroom with a walnut suite and a large bed, with a pale-blue shiny eiderdown in the centre of which lay Gladsome. Because Mrs. Woods had alluded to the hound as he and him, both Laurence and I had expected to see Spendthrift, and when we saw Gladsome instead, we were taken by surprise. Neither of us could think of anything to say. There was an awkward silence, while we collected our wits; then I said: "Oh, doesn't she look sweet?" And immediately wished I hadn't spoken.

"I don't know about sweet," said Mrs. Woods. "He's certainly made a mess of my eiderdown."

"I'm terribly sorry," apologised Laurence.

"I thought Mr. Dashwood was coming," said Mrs. Woods in dissatisfied accents. "At least I was led to believe he was."

"I'm Mr. Dashwood," said Laurence, trying to sound impressive, but failing dismally.

"What, the Master?" asked Mrs. Woods.

"That's right," I said.

"Come on, Gladsome," said Laurence, dragging her off the bed. "I'm sorry she troubled you, Mrs. Woods.

I can promise it won't occur again."

We walked downstairs in silence. Then Laurence and I apologised again and thanked Mrs. Woods for ringing us, and ran down the crazy-paving stones just as Daddy started to hoot the horn impatiently.

Laurence muttered about his age, while Daddy drove swiftly to Long Chill Farm. He said that he would soon be driven to making his hair grey with flour, or wearing a wig, or smoking a manly pipe, or wearing a suit. Gladsome sat on my knee and looked out of the window. I was too sleepy to talk. I wondered whether Andrew was still cross and what he would say about my being lost all day. Daddy told Laurence not to worry about his age and reminded him that Pitt was Prime Minister at twenty-one.

The Days were very surprised when we drove into the farmyard. Kate saw our arrival out of a window. She waved frantically and a second later we heard her shrieking: "Quick, quick, the Dashwoods are here. They've just turned up in their car. Something exciting must have happened."

"Why should our visit foretell excitement?" asked Daddy. "Do they always behave like this when you arrive?"

I explained that Kate was excited because it was late and we had turned up in the car.

Laurence said: "She's an optimist. She's always expecting good news. But what she means by good news I have never been able to discover."

The back door slammed and Kate and Harry came racing towards us. Valentine and Andrew were following more sedately behind.

"If you are more than ten minutes I shall go without you," threatened Daddy, as we stepped out of the car.

"Okay," I said, calling Gladsome.

"Oh, where did you find her?" shrieked Kate.

"Hallo, have you come back to the land of the living?" asked Andrew, grinning at me. "You don't mean to say you've been looking for Gladsome all the time."

"Yes, ever since twelve," I answered, pleased to find that Andrew wasn't angry.

"No, honestly, where did you find her?" asked Kate.

"At six o'clock on an eiderdown," said Laurence.

"No, seriously," said Valentine. "Was she in Ashbury Wood or down in that messy little osier bed?"

"She was on a posh eiderdown on a bed in a semi-detached house in Buckingham Drive, if you know where that is," said Laurence.

It was some time before the Days believed our story. Then they all laughed, and Andrew said that his whippers-in would have to keep an eye on Gladsome in future. Valentine said that it was a good thing Mrs. Woods wasn't really disagreeable, because it would have been dreadful if she had made us pay the laundry bill. Kate said that if Gladsome was a person she would have a boy and a girl and call them Neat and Sweet, and make them wear pale-blue ribbon in their hair.

We put Gladsome into the largest lodging-room and Andrew told us that Spendthrift had come strolling into the kennel-yard about half an hour ago, looking as though he owned the place; which pleased us, because it meant all hounds were in kennel. Then Andrew asked me how I had lost hounds, and I told my story.

When I had finished Andrew said that he had never meant me to go to the end of the wood, but only to the end of the track and that I should never go so far that I couldn't hear the horn or hounds. I said I was sorry and that I was really rather half-witted, and Andrew said I wasn't to make a mountain out of a molehill, and that everyone was lost at some time or other.

Valentine said: "I bet every huntsman loses his whips once in a lifetime."

"And I bet he sacks them when he does," said Kate.

"If only it hadn't happened at the opening meet," I said.

"Well, we all knew something would go wrong," said Andrew. "It would have been much worse if we'd had a blank day. At least everyone can say now, well, they may lose their whippers-in sometimes, but, by George, they hunt."

"It's nice to have a sort of mad reputation," said Valentine. "It gives you so much scope."

"You wait till I get lost and you have to hunt hounds, Sandy," said Andrew.

"I bet the field says something then," I said, trying to imagine myself casting hounds, putting them into covert, blowing the "gone-away."

"Daddy will say something if we don't go in a moment," said Laurence.

"He's hooting now," I said, hearing the car horn. "Come on, we had better run."

"See you tomorrow," shouted Valentine.

"And don't bother about having been lost," shouted Andrew.

"Happy dreams!" yelled Kate.

"You really are inconsiderate," said Daddy as Laurence and I fell into the car. "I'm practically frozen to my seat."

We apologised as we turned for home, and I thought how nice the Days were and that I had better improve my horn-blowing, because one day Andrew might get lost, and it would be dreadful if I couldn't even blow the horn properly.

SEVEN

The day after the opening meet it snowed. We didn't take hounds out, and Laurence and I only walked Overture and Daystar down to the end of the drive and back.

We spent the afternoon at Long Chill Farm discussing the Farmers' Dinner.

Colonel Hayward had told everyone at the opening meet that we were having a dinner, so now we had to have one whether we liked the idea or not. Laurence wasn't very pleased. He was sure it would cost more money than we could afford. But Kate and Andrew were all for it, and so was Mr. Day. Andrew had already written a list of the people to invite. At the top were the people he thought would subscribe towards the cost of the dinner, as well as coming. It was like this:

Colonel Hayward Mr. Austin-Smith Mr. Brooks Mr. Day	will subscribe

Mr. Watson } might subscribe
Mr. Smythe }

Mr. Tegg (probably won't come)

and Mr. Day had added:

Mr. Long Jackson
Mr. Harris

Laurence looked at the list for some time. Then he said: "And how much do you think the top people will subscribe?"

"Well, Colonel Hayward's promised twenty pounds and Dad's promised the same. I should think Mr. Brooks is good for a tenner and Mr. Austin-Smith for fifty at least" said Andrew.

"Fantastic," said Laurence.

"Colonel Hayward wants us to hold it in that hotel near Melcham. What's it called?" said Andrew.

"The White Lion," answered Valentine. "Apparently he had a dinner there once, I can't remember what for, and they charged only ten pounds a head including drinks and it was super."

"It sounds as though everything's about settled," said Laurence.

"We've still got to design the invitation cards," said Valentine.

"Why aren't we asking Mrs. Simmons?" I inquired.

"Because Farmers' Dinners are not meant for women," said Andrew.

"Isn't it unfair?" cried Kate, who had obviously discussed the subject before.

"But what about us, Kate and Valentine and me?" I asked, suddenly realising how much I was looking forward to the dinner already and how awful it would be if I couldn't go after all.

"Oh, they have to have the whippers-in and the secretary," said Andrew. "But I think you'll have to go before the end."

"How mean," said Kate.

"We'll only be bored if we stay," said Valentine. "After dinner they all tell stories and long, dull hunting anecdotes. I bet it's frightfully dull."

"We've forgotten the cigars," said Andrew.

"Ugh! You don't mean to say we've all got to smoke cigars?" said Kate.

"Of course not," said Andrew. "But lots of people like one after a good dinner."

"Well, you needn't get one for me," said Laurence.

"Do we really have to have them?" asked Kate. "It seems such an awful waste of money and supposing everyone smokes two."

"They won't," said Andrew.

"I thought we agreed to do the dinner properly, or not have one at all," said Valentine, rather crossly. "It's traditional to have cigars at a Farmer's Dinner. We can't possibly not have them."

"That's settled then," said Laurence.

"I think we'll have to invite someone else if Mr. Tegg doesn't come," said Valentine.

"I bet Mr. Watson subscribes a few pounds" said Kate. "He's pretty generous when all's said and done."

"Of course, we may find it works out at more than ten pounds a head," said Andrew. "A lot depends on what drinks we have."

"When are you thinking of holding it?" asked Laurence.

"We thought we would have it in December," said Andrew. "On the second Saturday. What do you think, Laurence?"

"Sounds all right to me," said Laurence.

"Tomorrow some of us had better go and see the White Lion then," said Andrew. "And see whether they can fix us up. Then we can have the cards printed."

"Oh, it does sound fun," said Kate. "I'm looking forward to it already. But what on earth shall I wear? I do hate dressing up. Can't I go in hunting kit?"

"Not possibly," said Andrew. "You'll have to wear a dress."

"But it's so unsuitable for a whip to wear a dress," cried Kate. "And all mine are too short anyway."

"Well, ask Mum to buy you a new one," said Andrew.

"I bet they all ask for brandies and double whiskies," said Kate, after a moment.

"Anyway, we can't really decide any more until we've seen the White Lion," said Andrew. "Laurence, Valentine and I can pop round tomorrow and find out everything."

And that's how we left it. Laurence and I returned to Little Hall; Laurence, I regret to say, still filled with misgiving.

The next day Valentine, Laurence and Andrew rode over to the White Lion and saw the manager. He showed them the dining-room, which was low and panelled, and offered to provide mushroom soup, turkey or chicken and three vegetables, and a choice of three sweets, and cheese, followed by coffee, for ten pounds a head. With drinks, he thought that it would work out at about fifteen a head, but he said he would prefer the drinks to be paid for separately rather than included in the overhead charge.

Apparently, the manager, who was called Mr. Temple, knew all about us and very soon said: "You come from the Chill Valley Hunt, don't you?"

He gave Valentine, Andrew and Laurence all cider on the house, and they came back feeling merry.

"Everything's easy now," Andrew told Kate and me. "We've booked the dinner for Friday, December the sixteenth, and arranged to have beer and a bottle of Scotch on the table, and port."

We talked a lot about the Farmers' Dinner during the next few days. The girls at my school were very envious when they heard about it; they grumbled and said that I had all the luck and couldn't I arrange a dinner for them. Mummy and Daddy were pleased when I told them, but not quite as pleased as I had expected them to be. Mummy said I was rather young to go to Farmers' Dinners, and Daddy said I could only go on one condition. Laurence was there at the time and he guessed what Daddy meant. "It's all right. Andrew's bringing Sandy, Valentine and Kate home when they start passing the port round," he said.

Mummy looked relieved, and Daddy said: "Mind he does."

On Saturday we hunted again. We met at Allate, on the green, and the whole village turned out to see us. Hounds looked like a Christmas card when they stood by Andrew, with the green and the trees in front of them, and the church and thatched cottages behind. The sun was shining and the day was warm and breezy.

We drew Mr. Hind's two coverts and found a fox. But he didn't run far—only to Hazel Wood where he went to ground in the side of an old pit. We left Kate behind to push sticks into the earth so that, if another fox ran that way, he couldn't go to ground, and drew Hazel Wood and Long Wood and a copse on Mr. Smythe's land. But we didn't find again and soon after three we decided to call it a day.

Mr. and Mrs. Brooks had invited us to meet at Little Bottom Farm on the next Saturday, and we all washed our breeches and spent hours poshing up our clothes during the week. But on Friday morning the police rang up and told the Days that there had been a case of foot-and-mouth disease on the other side of Hettington, and that we were within the fourteen-mile radius, and wouldn't be able to hunt or exercise hounds for a fortnight. The Days were furious, but there was nothing we could do. We rang up the Brooks and discovered that they knew already and had cancelled the cakes and sausage-rolls ordered for the meet. We spent Saturday tidying the boiler-house and the Days' saddle-room, and taking the horses for a long ride.

We sent invitations to the Farmer's Dinner to all the people on Andrew's list and, except for Mr. Tegg, everyone accepted. Mr. Austin-Smith sent a donation of twenty-five pounds and Mr. Watson came to see us on a Sunday and, after talking for hours, gave us a fiver towards the dinner.

The last leaves fell from the trees and December came, and still we couldn't hunt because of foot-and-mouth disease. The days dragged, each seeming to pass more slowly than the last, and there were hard frosts, bright starlit nights, sharp, clear invigorating days, and days when the snow lay across the valley and we seemed shut away from the rest of the world in our own muffled white hemisphere.

We started to talk about Christmas shopping, and Mummy ordered the turkey and we made our Christmas pudding. We had clipped the horses before the opening meet; but their coats had grown since then and now they looked patchy. Andrew said that they must be clipped again before Boxing Day, when the meet was to be in front of Hettington Town Hall, by invitation of the Mayor. We were all very excited about the Boxing Day meet and we talked of little else but that and the Farmers' Dinner.

Hettington Town Hall is in the Market Place and we all knew there would be a large crowd to watch us when we met there. Andrew and Laurence raced around in the landrover seeing nearby farmers so that, with any luck, we would have a good day over a completely new piece of country.

Unless there was another case of foot-and-mouth in Flosshire we were clear to hunt where we liked any day after December the sixteenth. We arranged two meets before Christmas—one on Saturday the seventeenth at Long Chill Farm and the other on Wednesday the twenty-first at Little Bottom Farm.

Everything was now arranged for the Farmers' Dinner and the Days turned their attention to the meet at Long Chill Farm. Mrs. Day thought the seventeenth was a very silly day for it, because, she said, they would all be tired and cross after the dinner. But Valentine and

Andrew said that it was the best possible place to meet after a late night, because, since they had no hack to the meet, they could have an extra half-hour in bed.

As the sixteenth drew near, Mrs. Day, Valentine and Kate visited Chidlington and bought dresses to wear at the dinner. Mummy said that my blue dress with white flowers would do beautifully, so I was spared a shopping expedition.

Mr. Day and Colonel Hayward advised Andrew and Laurence endlessly on Farmers' Dinners, and Laurence learned that he would have to make some sort of speech, thanking the guests for coming, as well as telling a funny story. Poor Laurence soon began to dread the dinner. Though he had been president of the Debating Society at his school and means to become a barrister, he insisted that he was hopeless at either public or after-dinner speaking and that he would stick, stammer, stutter and turn red and embarrass everyone else and be a misery to himself. He tried to pass the job on to Andrew, but Andrew only laughed and said he knew his place and that huntsmen were not expected to make speeches at Farmers' Dinners. In vain Laurence argued that Andrew was not a professional huntsman and therefore perfectly entitled to address the guests. Andrew was stubborn and, although everyone told Laurence he need only say a few words, he continued to worry.

I had to go to school as usual on the morning of the Farmers' Dinner, because my school didn't break up until the nineteenth; but I might just as well have stayed at home, because I could think of nothing but the evening.

I imagined the guests arriving one by one and I

hoped that their first words wouldn't be, "How many brace have you killed this season?" because I didn't think that a brace and a half sounded nearly enough. I hoped, too, that they wouldn't slap Laurence on the back and call him "my boy," or "son," because I knew if they did he would be upset for the rest of the evening. I hoped Valentine, who was in charge of the seating arrangements, would put me next to someone to whom it would be easy to talk.

The teachers were maddened by my lack of attention. Miss Timpson, the gym mistress, said I spoilt the whole lesson and, "Why was it I couldn't keep in time with the rest of the class?" I hadn't heard her say, "Now all together, girls, up, down," because at that moment, I was seeing everyone sitting down in the dim, panelled dining-room at the White Lion. Waiters were moving back chairs, and Laurence was wondering when to speak. Miss Timpson's cross voice brought me back to reality with a jerk, and I'm afraid I giggled. Keeping in time with the rest of the class seemed so very unimportant compared with all that was at stake in the evening. But Miss Timpson didn't know anything about the Farmers' Dinner. She thought I was laughing at her and she wasn't at all pleased. She told me that I should have to stay in during break and that she was surprised I hadn't better manners, and that I must remember that I was quite a big girl now and try to be my age. I was most upset to hear that I was quite a big girl now; unlike Laurence, I hate the thought of growing up and I'm terrified of becoming too heavy for Daystar.

But at last school was finished and I met Valentine and Kate and Harry by the station, and we travelled home together in the bus. Harry would hardly speak, because he thought he should come to the dinner and none of the Days would let him. Kate was in a silly mood and would only giggle. Valentine was worrying about introducing people the right way round and wondering whether she would know Mr. Harris from Mr. Long Jackson.

Soon, I gave up trying to talk to any of them. I looked out of the window and, once again, I hunted across the familiar countryside on Daystar, jumping an endless succession of fences, cutting wire, opening gates, only this time it was slightly different from usual—this time, it was me who was hunting hounds.

Valentine prodded me when we reached our stop. "Wake up," she said. "Or don't you want to come to the Farmers' Dinner?"

Laurence was pressing his dark suit when I reached home. I ate tea and then I had a bath, and changed and asked Mummy if I looked all right. She said, "turn round," and "stand up straight," and "don't stoop." Then she said I looked sweet and very nice and about ten years old; which I thought was very tactless of her as I had spent hours at her dressing-table powdering my nose and trying to make myself look at least seventeen.

Laurence appeared a few minutes later in his dark suit and one of Daddy's ties. He looked unusually clean and even younger than usual.

"Oh, I do feel smug and respectable," he said, glaring angrily at the crease in his trousers. "Don't you think I would look better in my ordinary clothes? I feel so townish in this outfit."

Mummy said: "You look very nice. You can't possibly wear that awful old hacking-jacket and your corduroy trousers to a Farmers' Dinner. You would disgrace the hunt, not to mention looking as though you hadn't a penny to your name."

Daddy laughed, and said: "Wait until you're in chambers, Laurence, and have to be respectable."

Laurence said: "I thought I was never going to get my cuff-links in. But we seem to be ready hours early, in spite of everything. The Days aren't calling till half-past seven and it's not seven yet."

"I bet they're in a flap," I said, imagining Kate struggling into her new dress and Andrew putting on a suit for the first time in years.

"Kate will have lost everything," said Laurence. "She'll be shrieking the house down. And she'll probably have suddenly got fatter in the night and won't be able to get into her new dress. Oh, I wish we had never arranged this wretched dinner. I know it's going to be a flop. My story doesn't sound funny any more and I'm rapidly losing my voice."

"At least, our parents aren't coming to watch us," I said, hoping to console Laurence. "Think of the Days with their father at their elbows all evening."

"He's coming late," said Laurence. "He may not even be in time for the actual dinner. He's got to see someone on important business first. That's why Valentine's in such a flap about knowing Mr. Long Jackson and Mr. Harris apart."

Laurence sat down wearily in one of the dining-room chairs. "Oh, why are we always ready so early?" he asked. "We've still got twenty minutes to wait before they even appear."

"Why don't you read a book?" asked Mummy. "I can't see what you're worrying about. You'll probably make a far better speech than most M.F.H.s do, and, if you do mix people up and introduce them the wrong way round, it's not a major tragedy."

Laurence picked up the evening paper which Daddy had brought home with him. "My speech will be the worst ever made in the history of Farmers' Dinners," he said.

I put on an overcoat and ran down the garden path and said good night to the horses. Daystar was sweet: she blew down my neck and nuzzled my pockets and agreed that hunt servants were not expected to distinguish themselves at dinners, and that it was their performance in the hunting-field which counted—which was actually poor comfort when I remembered the last few times I had hunted.

I wandered indoors again and found that Laurence had deserted the evening paper and was now pressing his overcoat, which he said was crumpled and which he had just discovered had a hole in one elbow. I realised that I had forgotten a handkerchief. While I was collecting one, I heard a car-horn outside the front gate. A second later Laurence was yelling: "Sandy, Sandy, do come on. They've arrived."

The Days all looked very smart, but rather uncomfortable and not at all like themselves. Andrew was wearing a brown double-breasted suit and no overcoat, which upset Laurence, who immediately took off his. Valentine was wearing a very smart black-and-white checked dress and a black overcoat belonging to her mother. Kate's new dress, which was being altered, hadn't arrived, much to her consternation and she was wearing her best summer one which, she said, was much too short and quite unsuitable. She had stuck a comb in her dark hair to try and make herself look older.

We all looked at each other for a moment, and then Kate said: "You do look smart, Sandy." I said: "I wouldn't know any of you if I met you in the middle of London."

Andrew said: "I have a message from my father for you, Laurence. It is: Stand up, Speak up, and Shut up."

"What a nice thing to hear at the last minute," said Valentine sarcastically.

"I'm prepared for the worst," said Laurence. "At least I know my audience won't boo."

We had reached Allate now and, beneath the moon, the green looked more beautiful to me than ever before. "You'll probably be a politician before you've done, Laurence," said Andrew. "Lots of barristers become M.P.s."

"Not quite my line of country," said Laurence.

At that moment the landrover let off a series of bangs, and Kate said: "Gosh!" Andrew said that a tyre must have burst and now we would all have to walk the rest of the way. He stopped the landrover, and Valentine said that she couldn't possibly walk because she had on her mother's best high-heeled shoes and she couldn't even walk upstairs much less a couple of miles along a country road. Kate said that she was wearing her only pair of tights, and she didn't mean to ladder them for anyone.

Andrew said: "What do you intend to do then? Sit here all night or do you expect Laurence and me to change the wheel in our best clothes?"

"You can take your coats off and we'll help," said Kate.

Andrew and Laurence got out, muttering. But when they looked at the tyres they found that they were all quite all right. We were very relieved and, as we drove on towards the White Lion we felt quite cheerful.

"I wish we could stay till the bitter end," said Kate.

"Who do you think will arrive first?" asked Andrew. "I'm betting on Mr. Smythe."

"I'm not. I'm sure Mr. Watson will be first," said Kate. "He's always early."

"I think either Mr. Long Jackson or Mr. Harris will be first," said Valentine. "Just because we don't know them apart and won't know which one it is."

"I'm betting on Mr. Austin-Smith," I said.

"I think Mr. – Mr.——' said Laurence, as we swung round the last corner and saw Colonel Hayward's car parked in front of the White Lion. "Colonel Hayward will be first," Laurence finished.

"Cheat," said Kate.

I looked at my watch and saw that it was ten to eight.

"We've allowed a quarter of an hour for drinks before dinner," said Andrew, parking the landrover.

The manager of the White Lion met us in the hall. He shook us all by the hand and showed us into the lounge, where we found Colonel Hayward drinking a whisky and soda. He insisted on treating us all to a drink. Laurence tried to argue, but the deed was done in a moment. Colonel Hayward was feeling cheerful. He had already discussed the dinner with the manager and knew exactly what was in store for us. He said: "I'm so glad you remembered the cigars and that everyone's coming. This evening is going to do you a lot of good, you know. It'll make local people sit up a bit."

There were horse brasses hanging round the fireplace and a row of pewter mugs along the bar. Kate, Valentine and I took off our coats. Andrew was talking to Colonel Hayward; Laurence was looking pale and desperate. Soon Mr. Austin-Smith and a strange man none of us knew arrived. Laurence looked helplessly at Valentine, but she obviously didn't know whether he was Mr. Long Jackson or Mr. Harris. Colonel Hayward saved the situation.

"Hallo, Frank," he said. "What will you drink? You know the Days, don't you? And our Master, Mr. Laurence Dashwood? This is Mr. Long Jackson, Laurence," he continued. "A very old friend of mine."

Laurence shook hands with Mr. Long Jackson, who was tall and dark and formidable, and said: "What will you drink?"

Mr. Long Jackson said: "I think the Colonel's ordered me one. Thanks all the same."

Laurence looked at Andrew. No one could think of anything to say. Then I said: "Do you live near Melcham?" At the same moment Valentine said: "Have you lived in the district long?"

Mr. Long Jackson laughed, and said: "Which shall I answer first?" Valentine and I felt stupid and embarassed. Kate was examining the horse brasses. Mr. Long Jackson said he lived three miles from Melcham and that much of his land adjoined Little Bottom Farm.

Mr. Brooks, Mr. Harris, Mr. Austin-Smith and Mr. Watson arrived. Mr. Brooks was wearing a sporting and rather loud, checked suit. Mr. Harris and Mr. Austin-Smith were wearing brown and blue lounge suits. Mr. Watson had on his usual hacking-jacket, breeches, knitted socks and boots. Colonel Hayward had treated them all to drinks before Laurence had finished shaking hands.

"Now, we only want Mr. Day and Mr. Smythe," said Colonel Hayward.

The lounge clock said ten past eight. Everyone seemed to be talking at the tops of their voices. Mr. Austin-Smith came across to where Kate and I were standing by the fire.

"And how are the invisible whips?" he asked, with a smile. "They missed a wonderful run on the day of the opening meet."

"I know, it was dreadful," said Kate.

"How did it happen?" asked Mr. Austin-Smith.

I explained and thought how foolish my story sounded, and hoped that everyone wouldn't ask me the same question.

Mr. Austin-Smith was very sympathetic. "It happens to everyone," he said. "And in woods like Ashbury Wood you can be right on top of hounds and not hear them. By the way, did you find the lost hounds?"

Kate and I told the story of Gladsome and the bed in Buckingham Drive, and, when Mr. Austin-Smith had finished laughing, he said: "I wish you would come and meet at my house again this season. The East Nightley show no signs of meeting nearer than five or six miles away, and I've a brace of foxes for certain in the gorse covert on the hill."

"Thank you very much, we'd love to," I said.

"Thanks awfully," said Kate.

Mr. Smythe had arrived. Colonel Hayward was buying him a drink. Laurence was talking to Mr. Harris and Mr. Long Jackson.

Mr. Austin-Smith said: "I've been wondering whether you would like to have a little mare I've had for some time. She's not up to my weight and she's a bit green and rather on the gassy side, but for anyone who can ride, she'll make a topping hunter."

"Well, it's awfully nice of you," said Kate. "But I'm afraid we can't afford to buy another just at the moment. You see, our finances aren't too good and we've got some heavy commitments to meet before the end of the season."

I hoped Laurence hadn't heard Kate's remarks. He hates the hunt's finances to be discussed in public, and he was looking our way.

"But I'm not interested in selling her," said Mr. Austin-Smith. "I bought her for a song a year or two ago and she's been turned out ever since. I thought I might get someone to ride her in a few point-to-points, but I've never had the time to get her fit. If you had her, she would be a present."

"Oh, but we'd love to have her," cried Kate, forgetting that she was in a hotel lounge full of people. "How big is she?"

Laurence scowled at me. I tried to catch Kate's eye, but she was far too excited to notice me.

"A little over fifteen hands," said Mr. Austin-Smith.

"She's in the book. I bought her from a racing stable as a three-year-old. She's five now and could win a hack class with a bit of schooling."

I thought that Mr. Austin-Smith must be exceptionally generous to give away such a nice mare.

"She's bay with two white socks and a star," he continued, "and she's called Lost Horizon. But I must warn you, she's not everyone's ride. She's hot and she doesn't know much."

I saw us schooling a beautiful bay thoroughbred, with dark kind eyes and a long, easy stride.

"Could we come over and try her some time?" I asked.

"Yes, if you like," said Mr. Austin-Smith rather reluctantly. "Personally, I think you had much better have her down at the farm for a week or ten days, and then let me know what you think of her. She needs handling."

"That would be marvellous," I said. "May we talk it over with the others and then give you a ring?"

"Certainly," said Mr. Austin-Smith. "Sleep on it. I don't want to rush you into anything you're going to regret afterwards."

Valentine was coming across the room towards us. "We're just going in to dinner," she said.

The long, low, panelled dining-room was lit by candles. The curtains were drawn and in the open fireplace a fire blazed. I expected to see Elizabethan ladies coming across the room to greet us. On the table the glasses were shining.

Valentine told me where to sit. Mr. Watson was on my left—between me and Kate—and on my right was

Mr. Smythe, the farmer who had been so unpleasant the previous season. He seemed unusually cheerful tonight.

"Well, how are you, young lady?" he inquired. "Killed many foxes this season?"

"A brace and a half," I answered, wishing I could name a more impressive figure. "But we've only hunted properly about twice because of foot-and-mouth."

"When are you coming over my land again?" he asked. "I've got an old dog fox in the copse near where you killed last season."

"Well, we're pretty well fixed up till the end of January," I said, remembering Mr. Austin-Smith's invitation.

"Better leave it till after the shooting's finished now," said Mr. Smythe. "You had best come and see me towards the end of February."

Farther down the table, the invisible whippers-in seemed to be the main topic of conversation. Everyone was laughing and I wondered whether Kate and I would ever live down our new name. We'll have to show them on Boxing Day, I thought, and tomorrow. Laurence was sitting at the head of the table. He wasn't looking worried any more. He was talking earnestly to Mr. Long Jackson. I started to eat the plate of mushroom soup in front of me. It was very good. I glanced at Valentine, sitting much farther down the table, and I thought she looked quite grown up. She was wearing a string of pearls and a bracelet; Andrew was discussing our puppies with Colonel Hayward. Suddenly there was a loud crash as Kate upset her soup. Two waiters rushed and collided with Mr. Watson, who had sprung to his feet. Kate turned bright scarlet and Andrew began to talk very loudly.

"Accidents will happen," said Mr. Watson, mopping at Kate with his napkin.

"He's a real blighter," said Mr. Smythe, who, I suddenly realised, was still talking about the fox in his copse. "Must be a son of the one you killed last season."

"Sounds like it," I agreed. The waiters began to take away the soup plates. Mr. Smythe helped himself liberally from the bottle of Scotch on the table. "All the best," he said, draining half a glass.

I hoped all the farmers wouldn't drink so much. I knew Laurence would have a fit, if we had to pay seven or eight pounds for another bottle of whisky. But on my other side Mr. Watson was asking for water or lemonade, and I thought, "what you lose on the roundabout you make up on the swings," and felt more cheerful.

I expected someone to make a speech, or, at least, propose a toast. But they only gulped their drinks, and said, "Cheers," or "Happy Christmas," or "Good hunting," or, like Mr. Smythe, "All the best."

I was disappointed. I had imagined someone springing to their feet, and crying: "Here's to the Chill Valley Foxhounds, long may they hunt our woods and valleys," and then everyone crying "Hear, hear," and clinking glasses and throwing back their drinks. The dinner suddenly seemed staid.

"Good stuff," said Mr. Smythe, smacking his lips and gulping down more whisky. "This'll keep the cold out."

I couldn't think of anything to say. Kate was looking

glum and decidedly damp. I helped myself to vegetables and started to eat the next course. Mr. Watson began to talk. "This dinner must be costing you a lot of money," he said, "though I should think this place is pretty reasonable as places go. I see there's going to be port too; that's expensive. Still, Mr. Temple's a very reasonable man. I know him well, you know. I used to stay here before I lived where I do now. He's a great friend of mine." I hoped the other guests couldn't hear Mr. Watson's ill-chosen remarks about the price of the dinner. "Did you think to mention my name?" he asked. "It would have made all the difference."

I knew that at any moment Mr. Watson would ask the price of the dinner. I wanted to change the subject, but could think of nothing to say. "Good thing they don't all drink like Mr. Smythe," said Mr. Watson, dropping his voice. "You would need half a dozen bottles of Scotch if they did, and that would cost a pretty penny."

"Yes, it would," I agreed, wondering whether Laurence had funked his speech or forgotten all about it.

"How much does it cost to-day?" asked Mr. Watson. "Ten pounds a bottle?"

"I don't know," I answered. "I don't really know an awful lot about drink, I'm afraid."

"You shouldn't; not at your age," said Mr. Watson. "I never touch the stuff myself."

"There was an earth there back in the summer," said Mr. Smythe, still talking about his copse, with the old dog fox in it. "But I got one of my men to fill it in. I don't know where he lies in now."

I wondered whether Mr. Smythe meant his man or the fox.

"My wife was the same," continued Mr. Watson. "Never touched it."

Mr. Smythe helped himself to some more whisky. "I shouldn't be surprised if we had a heavy fall of snow next month," he said.

"How are you feeling?" asked Mr. Watson, addressing Kate. "It didn't scald you, did it?"

They had already started to tell stories farther along the table. People began to eat peach melba, ice-cream and trifle. Andrew was looking at Kate and me rather hard. I guessed he wanted us to eat up and be ready to go quite soon. Someone was asking Laurence how many foxes we had killed last season. Laurence evaded a direct answer. He said that we had accounted for so many—I couldn't hear the exact number. I started to eat peach melba.

Mr. Smythe said: "And how large is your pack now, young lady?" For an awful moment I couldn't remember; then I said: "Thirteen couple including the puppies." He looked at me rather hard, and said: "That's not very many for a country like this. I'm not surprised you don't kill many foxes." I decided that I didn't like Mr. Smythe very much and that Farmers' Dinners were an overrated form of entertainment. Farther along people started to eat some sort of savoury on toast, and biscuits and cheese. I realised that Kate and I would miss Laurence's speech. Andrew was making frantic faces in our direction. It was obvious that he wanted us to leave very soon now. But the waiters hadn't cleared away our sweet plates yet and I was determined to try the cheese. So I avoided Andrew's eye, and said: "I expect we'll kill many more this season and still more next season when our young hounds start to hunt."

Kate's took some cheese at the same moment as she caught Andrew's eye, and in trying to be quick she upset the salt. She looked very embarassed; Mr. Watson came to her rescue and hastily started to scrape up the spilled salt with his cheese knife. I winked at Kate in an effort to make her feel more cheerful. Laurence was looking at me very hard now. I wished we had discussed Kate and my leaving before the end much more fully. I gobbled my cheese and wondered whether I should just stand up, and bid my friends on each side farewell, and go, or wait until Andrew or Laurence made a move. Then Mr. Day arrived and while he was shaking everyone by the hand, Valentine and Andrew came across and said: "Come on, it's time to go home."

Valentine, Kate and I said good-bye to everyone in turn.

Mr. Austin-Smith said: "Good-bye, '*fair girls on grey horses*,' let me know about the mare."

Colonel Hayward said: "Time you went. Grand dinner. Good night."

Mr. Smythe said: "Remember my meet, young lady, and best of luck on Boxing Day."

Everyone else just said "Good night," or "Good-bye," and shook us by the hand.

It was very cold outside. The night was still moonlit and the grass and trees were tipped with white. "Hope it thaws before tomorrow or we won't be able to hunt," said Andrew.

Kate shivered. "Wasn't I awful?" she said. "Upsetting

my soup and then the salt?"

"It doesn't matter," said Andrew, starting up the landrover. "Those sort of things happen to everyone."

"I'm jolly glad I hadn't got my new dress on," said Kate.

"I liked Mr. Long Jackson," said Valentine. "He wants us all to go to tea one day and meet his children. Apparently the son's been out hunting with us once or twice."

"When's Laurence going to make his speech?" I asked. "Or has he forgotten?"

"He's probably making it now," said Andrew, driving faster.

Andrew dropped me first, so I didn't really have a chance to discuss the Farmers' Dinner properly with the Days until after hunting on the next day. But Mummy and Daddy were still up and longing to hear all about it. They were sorry I hadn't heard Laurence's speech and they agreed that Kate's mishaps were tiresome, but of no lasting significance.

That night I dreamed that Laurence made his speech in a top hat and that he was wearing spats. He thanked our guests for coming and then gave a long discourse on poetry which was received in gloomy silence. Some time in the early hours of the next morning I wakened with a start and realised that Laurence had just arrived home and was moving about in his room next door.

I shrieked: "Hallo, how did the speech go off?" Laurence said: "Ssh," and crept along the passage. Looking into my room, he said: "Not too badly, thank you. Everyone clapped a lot, anyway, and Colonel Hayward made a very complimentary speech back. I wished it had been someone else, though. Colonel Hayward's all right, but I wish he wouldn't be quite so organising. Honestly, you'd think he had arranged the whole thing, the way he went on at the end."

"Jolly annoying," I said, trying to sound interested, because I wanted to hear a great deal more about the dinner, though sleep was gradually overpowering me.

"You should have heard the noise at the end," said Laurence. "I'm sure everyone enjoyed themselves like anything. Certainly Mr. Day did. The trouble was, he became so boastful about his children. I'm quite sure now that he was the person who gave all those awful details to the Show on Bank Holiday. And did they all drink a lot of port and whisky?"

I knew Laurence was about to tell me how much it would all cost. I didn't want to stay awake any longer. I heard him say "one hundred pounds" and then I fell asleep. This time to dream of hunting in a forty-mile-an-hour gale on Mr. Austin-Smith's bay thoroughbred, which pulled with her head between her knees and kicked Vampire.

EIGHT

The Days were very excited about the meet at their house, and although it was the day after the Farmers' Dinner, they were all up by six o'clock.

Laurence and I rose early, too. We had become much quicker at plaiting and grooming our horses for hunting, and we were riding towards Long Chill Farm by ten o'clock. We found Kate and Harry rushing about the house with plates of eats in their hands. Mrs. Day was turning claret into mulled claret on the kitchen range. Valentine was arranging anchovies on slices of eggs and putting them on squares of toast. The horses stood ready in their boxes; Andrew was dressing upstairs. Laurence and I, having put Daystar and Overture into spare boxes, carried bottles of beer from the larder, and arranged glasses on the sideboard in the dining-room. Mrs. Day was worried because the four dozen cakes she had ordered from the local baker hadn't arrived. Laurence offered to fetch them in the landrover. For some time he had been having irregular and rather unorthodox driving lessons from Andrew. Mrs. Day hesitated, and then said: "Yes, all right. But for goodness' sake mind the policeman."

Laurence started up the landrover and at that moment the cakes arrived. He said a word we're not allowed to use and turned the engine off. Then, to our horror, we saw a crowd of horsemen coming along the lane, followed by Mr. Austin-Smith's trailer. I gave a cry of dismay, and, glancing at my watch, discovered that it was a quarter to eleven.

Laurence said: "I'll fetch the horses out." I rushed into the Days' kitchen, yelling: "There's lots of people coming and it's a quarter to eleven!"

Valentine shouted: "Keep calm," from the top of the stairs.

Kate shrieked: "I've starched my tie too much and now my pin won't go in. It just bends."

Andrew shouted: "Mum, Mum, have you seen my socks?"

At that moment the horsemen invaded the small gravel sweep in front of the house. Mr. Austin-Smith drew up outside the back door in his trailer, and Kate wailed: "It's always like this when you get up too early and there's plenty of time. It always makes you late."

Laurence was leading Mulligatawny up and down the lane by the kennel-yard. Bert Saunders was standing ready at the draw-yard gate. Mrs. Day found Andrew's socks and then rushed downstairs to help Mr. Day receive the guests.

Andrew called me and said: "What on earth does Laurence think he's doing leading Mulligatawny up and down the lane? Doesn't he know he's Master? He should be indoors talking politely, not leading the hunt servants' horses about."

"But it's getting so late," I said. "Surely we should all be mounted by now?"

"Not at all," said Andrew. "There's no earthly reason why hounds should appear a minute before eleven."

Andrew disappeared. I decided that late hours and early rising didn't suit him. Then I ran outside and told Laurence to give Mulligatawny to me and to go inside and talk politely to the guests. Three minutes later, Andrew, Valentine and Kate appeared, all looking very hot in spite of the cold day.

"It's hardly suitable for hunting," said Andrew, kicking the ground. "It's beginning to thaw, though, so it should be all right in another half an hour or so, but for goodness' sake go carefully. Don't turn quickly or gallop across plough, and look out for grassy patches. We don't want any accidents."

"Okay, chief," said Kate.

By now there were a dozen or more horses assembled in the lane outside the house. The Haywards had come and the Brooks with their children, and Jane Browne and Roger Wilcox and a large crowd from the riding school near Melcham. We fetched our horses and mounted; Bert Saunders let hounds out, and the sky cleared and there was a pale yellow sun shining on the white-tipped landscape. Spendthrift made a bee-line for the back door. Kate turned him back. Mummy and Daddy and Quinky arrived. Mummy called: "You look just like a Christmas card." Daddy said: "Do we go in?"

Andrew showed them the way round by the front door. Mr. Watson appeared and said: "How do you feel this morning?" and laughed and subjected us to the usual examination. Kate was hauled over the coals: her left spur was not resting on its stop and her right boot's tab was showing. Valentine brought us mulled wine and delicious eats on a tray.

"Everyone's talking like mad inside," she said. "They love the hot wine. Mr. Austin-Smith's had three glasses already."

The day was very bright now. It was like one of those sharp, clear, sheerly beautiful mornings which belong to early January.

"There won't be much scent," said Andrew. "Why can't it be warm and wet with a south-west wind and a cloudy sky?"

Half an hour later we were drawing Badger's Wood, then Poacher's Copse, then Hazel Wood and Long Wood, but all without success. Andrew was worried. For the first time in the annals of the Chill Valley Foxhounds Mr. Day had come out. He was riding his roan cob, Pink Gin, and because he was with us Andrew was particularly anxious that we should have a good day. Hounds were not behaving very well. Spendthrift wandered about on his own, looking superior, as though he thought himself above such tasks as foxhunting. Wasteful and Tell Tale hunted rabbits industriously. True Love followed the field.

"I suppose it's because they haven't hunted for so long," said Kate, returning from a rubbish-dump three fields away, where Gladsome and Tomboy had been enjoying themselves.

We were trotting towards Old Copse, a large wood on the edge of Mr. Hunt's land, and although it was only half-past one, already the field was much smaller. The contingent from the riding school at Melcham had gone home and so had the Brooks and their two children. Andrew told me to ride about a hundred yards ahead of him on the left side. I had hardly entered the wood when I heard a yelp and Laurence yelling: "Move that pony."

I wondered whether to go back. Andrew had halted. "You had better go on," he shouted. "Someone's ridden over Pick, but I don't think she's too badly hurt."

We found a fox in Old Copse, but hours seemed to pass before he broke. He was a big, light-coloured fox, and he came out just ahead of me and, looking very unconcerned, loped away towards Mr. Smythe's farm. I felt the thrill I always feel when I see a fox. For once I was in the right place at the right time. I felt very efficient. I blew my whistle and watched him slip through a wire fence at approximately ten yards from an oak tree. I blew my whistle again, and thought: "Pride comes before a fall; now be sensible, Sandy Dashwood." Andrew was galloping towards me. I could hear him crashing through the undergrowth in Old Copse. If only we can have a good day, I thought. If only Kate and I don't get lost.

"Which way did he go?" yelled Andrew.

"I turned Daystar's head towards the oak tree and waved my hat in the same direction. Andrew called hounds out. Somewhere behind, Kate was sending the laggards on. Dainty picked up the line, then Wasteful, Willing and True Love, and then suddenly the rest of the pack. They were all on. I counted them as they came out. Andrew was blowing the "gone-away." I yelled: "All on," to Kate. The next moment I was galloping on towards a gate in the wire fence. Above, the pale sun was still shining. The trees and grass were no longer tipped with white. I could hear the thunder of hoofs behind, and ahead the wonderful music of a pack in full cry rang through the dry, hard meadows. I opened the gate, which was padlocked, by lifting it off its hinges. I left it for the field to shut.

"A change to see Spendthrift hunting," shouted Andrew. "Perhaps he's going to mend his ways at last."

Hounds had reached another wood by now. They were hunting much more slowly.

"Slip round the far side," Andrew told me. "You might see a fox. But don't go too far and get lost again."

I had to take down a lot of wire before I could reach the far side of the wood. It was a maddening task. The spikes on the wire seized hold of my gloves at every opportunity, and, when I took them off, the wire tore my hands. Daystar was frantic. She was certain we would be lost again. She banged me on the back and pushed me into the wire at regular intervals. At last we were through, but unfortunately there was no sign of the field, so I still had to put the wire up again, while Daystar became more hysterical each moment and hounds hunted farther and farther into the wood. I had just mounted, when Kate came galloping towards me, crying: "Where can I get through?"

I was too angry with Providence to speak. I pointed to the wire which I had so laboriously put up, and galloped on. I was too late to see the fox, but I was able to count hounds as they came out of the wood in full cry. Andrew appeared a moment later. He jumped a stile out of the wood and then we galloped on together. "Where in the dickens is the field?" he asked. "I haven't seen them since we left Old Copse."

"I haven't either," I said.

"Well, here comes Kate anyway," said Andrew. "Hounds hunted magnificently through the wood. You should have seen the way True Love was throwing his tongue. He'll be a grand hound next season."

Ahead of us was a gate and stile giving access to a ploughed field. I wanted to jump the stile, but when we reached it we found the ground was hard and poached on both sides, and, before I had time to think, Andrew had opened the gate.

Kate had joined us by now. "Shovel's still in Old Copse," she said. "I couldn't get him out."

"Have you seen the field?" asked Andrew, shutting the gate and mounting.

"No, not for ages," answered Kate. "I can't think where they've got to."

"I'll give them a blow," said Andrew, and, putting his words into action, he blew the "gone-away." "They must have heard that," he said, pushing his horn back between the buttons on his coat.

We galloped on together. Kate said: "Shouldn't I be on the down-wind side?" And Andrew said: "It doesn't matter for the moment. I don't want to lose any whips today," and grinned.

Hounds were hunting towards a thick hedge fringed with gorse. Farther ahead we could see the river Lapp and bleak river meadows, and an occasional forlorn willow tree. Hounds seemed to lose their fox altogether when they reached the gorse. One moment they were in full cry and the next they were silently feathering backwards and forwards around the hedge.

"I reckon he's gone to ground," said Andrew. "How annoying." He dismounted and gave me his reins, just as Wasteful marked our fox to ground in an earth amid the gorse.

Andrew blew "gone to ground," and said: "If we hadn't lost the terriers we might have tried bolting him."

Kate said: "This is a funny sort of end without the field or anyone else. They won't be able to laugh at us any more, Sandy. They'll be the invisible ones in future."

I didn't say anything. I was thinking of Laurence and hoping it wasn't his fault the field were missing.

Andrew blew "gone to ground' again. Then he blew "home" and mounted Mulligatawny, and said: "It's a pity Dad missed the run. I bet he's furious."

The pale sun had disappeared from the sky. Evening was approaching across the empty fields. There was frost in the air; soon there would be a moon and cold, golden stars in a dark sky.

"Home," said Andrew.

Daystar wasn't tired. She wanted to trot home, and when I wouldn't let her, she jogged and went sideways.

I hoped Laurence wasn't in despair. Already I was imagining my homecoming. Laurence sunk in the deepest gloom; Overture in her loose box, rugged and bandaged.

Andrew handed me his horn. "See if you can blow 'Come away back home,'" he said, "or 'across the ride.'"

Kate and I practised horn-blowing most of the way

home. Hounds were merry and not at all tired. They were ahead of Andrew all the way, with sterns high.

"To-morrow the first of the puppies come home," said Andrew. "I want them all back by Christmas."

"I shall have to go shopping on Monday," said Kate. "I haven't got one single present yet."

The valley looked cold and bleak and beautiful beneath the moon. The kennel-yard was full of shadows. One of them belonged to Valentine. She was leaning against the draw-yard gate, her head in her hands.

"She's still in her hunting kit," said Kate as we drew near. "She can't have been back long."

I thought of Laurence searching empty fields, riding desperately through woods with an angry, muttering crowd of horsemen behind him; and then at last turning for home, the final good-nights and the hack to the kennels with Valentine and Mr. Day. My troubles on the day of the opening meet seemed small in comparison.

"I bet she's fed up," said Andrew. "And I bet Laurence, true to Dashwood temperament, is in despair."

Valentine waved as we reached the yard.

"Had a good day?" she called.

"Fine," said Andrew. "What happened to you?"

Valentine explained briefly while we put hounds away. Apparently Laurence had been unable to find a way out of Old Copse. He had led the field round and round for quite ten minutes, and when eventually he found a gap in the wire fence near where we had first entered, hounds had vanished.

"He's in a terrible state," said Valentine. "You know what Laurence is. He hates catastrophe."

It was cold riding along the hard, dry track to Little

Hall. I thought about Christmas, and decided that I would buy Laurence a sporting print and Andrew a checked tie. As I expected, I found Overture rugged and bandaged in her box. She was still plaited, though, and I guessed that Laurence was in his bath and had decided to cut her plaits out later.

I settled Daystar. Mummy was in the dining-room. She wanted to know all about my day.

Laurence, she said, was in his bath and completely disheartened. I told Mummy about finding the fox in Old Copse and about the run and his going to ground in the gorse.

Later, Laurence and I had tea together. He said: "To-day has been the worst day of my life. It was dreadful. I'm sure no one will ever trust me again."

In vain I told him that when hounds were running the field was perfectly entitled to choose its own line; in fact, from the moment Andrew blew the "gone-away" until the next check they were no longer his responsibility. He was determined to be gloomy. Finally I persuaded him to ring up Andrew. They talked for half an hour, and, when they had finished, Laurence grinned and seemed more cheerful.

The next day we had a long discussion about our reputation. We all agreed that it must be sinking fast.

"First the whips and then the Master gets lost," said Kate. "It's terrible."

"We'll be the laughing-stock of Flosshire soon." said Laurence sadly.

"We've just had one stroke of bad luck after another," said Valentine. "Personally, I think that dreadful speech at that frightful show on Bank Holiday was the worst thing which has happened to us this year."

"There's no doubt we've got to be brilliant next Saturday and on Boxing Day," said Andrew.

"Well, don't let's get up too early on Saturday morning," said Valentine. "If we go to bed at eleven and get up at five, of course, we can't be competent hunt servants. We're much too tired."

"I quite agree," said Laurence.

"I don't," said Kate. "Hurrying tires you much more than getting up a few hours earlier."

"Well, I'm not getting up before seven to please anyone," said Laurence. "We won't need to start before half-past nine and it only takes me an hour to get Overture ready."

"What about breakfast and dressing?" I said.

"Five minutes," said Laurence.

"Verger and Victor are coming back to-day," said Andrew. "Colonel Hayward's bringing them over at lunch-time."

"I can't see why you're so eager to have the puppies back," said Laurence. "It'll mean a great many more mouths to feed, and we're far from rich."

"But we must get to know them," said Andrew.

Getting to know the puppies was very exhausting. Victor and Verger were comparatively well trained. But the others, Vagabond, Villain, Viking, Venus, Vanity and Vision were far from well-behaved.

We took them exercising with the older hounds on Monday. But though we coupled them together and only took them up the lane, we were soon in trouble.

Vanity and Vision sat down by the duck-pond and refused to go any farther. Andrew said that we mustn't even show them our whips and that this was the crucial moment in their lives, and, if we disheartened them now, they would never be any good. Meanwhile, Vagabond and Villain dashed into the kitchen, and Viking and Venus each managed to get a different side of a fence. Andrew dismounted and talked to Vanity and Vision. Kate pursued Vagabond and Villain. Valentine and Laurence held the horses, and I persuaded Viking and Venus to return to the lane. Vanity and Vision continued to sit looking sheepish by the duck-pond, and Vagabond and Villain each ran round one side of a table leg in the kitchen. There was a sickening crash as the table overturned. Kate screamed: "Help, help! It's killing them!" At the same moment Wasteful and Tomboy saw a hare, and the pack disappeared across the valley in full cry.

Andrew said a word Laurence and I are not allowed to use, and Villain suddenly flew at Vagabond. Andrew separated them with difficulty. In the kitchen Kate was standing up the table again. A heap of broken crockery lay on the ground. Villain and Vagabond sat dismally surveying the scene.

"We had better try and get the young hounds back into kennel," said Andrew. "And then go in search of the pack."

Vanity and Vision were very temperamental and it took me ages to get them into the draw-yard. Valentine and Laurence put the horses away and helped collect the rest of the young hounds. Then we mounted our horses again and started to search for the pack. Fortunately they hadn't gone far. Andrew blew the horn, and one by one they came back across the valley.

"We'll have to teach the young hounds how to go in

couples before we take them out again," said Andrew.

"Mummy's furious about the state of the kitchen," said Kate.

"I'm not surprised," said Valentine.

"Fate's against us," said Kate. "One of us must have broken a mirror, or looked at a new moon through glass, or walked under a ladder without crossing our fingers. It'll be terrible if we're in for seven years of bad luck."

"It'll finish us," said Laurence gloomily.

After we had collected our pack and they were all safely installed in the lodging-rooms, we discussed the meet at Little Bottom Farm on the day after the morrow.

"Everybody's to keep very near me all day," said Andrew. "I'll soon shout if you press hounds. Fortunately, most of Mr. Brooks' coverts are small, so you should be able to stay outside and still see me. But if we don't find early and have to draw some of those big woods towards Chidlington, stick near me on the rides."

"Okay," said Laurence. "I've got no wish to be lost again."

"I shall probably do something silly," said Valentine. "I shall lose all the caps or offend our subscribers by trying to cap them."

"I hope the Brooks provide cherry brandy," said Kate.

"You're just a disgrace," said Andrew.

On Tuesday we took the young hounds out in couples. We didn't take more than two couple at a time and they behaved much better. In the evening we cleaned our hunting-kit again, and Kate grumbled horribly because she said only a few hours seemed to have passed since she was last cleaning it. Andrew said that she had better try whipping-in to a pack which hunted six days a week, then she *would* have something to talk about, and Kate said that probably the stable-boys did it for you then, or you had six pairs of breeches and boots.

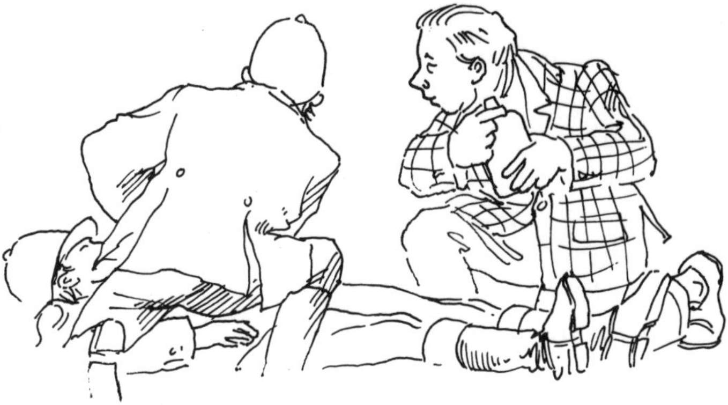

NINE

The meet at Little Bottom Farm did not rise to our expectations. We arrived a few minutes early and found the yard deserted. It was a bleak day. In the night there had been a frost, but now cold rain was falling and a sharp wind whistled round the farm buildings.

We could see Mr. and Mrs. Brooks' hunters looking over their box doors, otherwise there was no sign of life at Little Bottom Farm.

"Well, I don't call this much of a meet," said Andrew, looking at his watch. "Only five minutes to go and no one here."

"I'm jolly cold," said Kate. "I wish I had brought my mack'."

"My hands are like big, frozen lumps of ice," complained Harry.

At that moment Mrs. Brooks appeared with a tray laden with beer and sausage-rolls.

"What a morning!" she said, giving us all beer. "It's not fit to be alive."

Kate's face fell. The beer was very cold. Andrew

poured half his away when Mrs. Brooks' back was turned.

I remembered the Days' hot wine.

Soon a few horsemen began to arrive. Most of them were wearing mackintoshes, but they still looked cold.

At a quarter past eleven, when we were all blue and shivering, Mr. Brooks appeared on his bay hunter and showed us the way to the first covert. It was still raining. The ground was wet and greasy, and I couldn't feel my feet any more.

"Slip on to the far corner," Andrew told me. "They stopped the earths last night, so you might see a fox."

Daystar was cold too. She pulled and my cold hands felt large and awkward.

The covert was small and we drew it blank. After that we tried some kale and I began to feel warmer, and it stopped raining. We drew the kale blank, too, and Andrew said: "This doesn't look very grand." Kate said: "I hope the Brookses *have* got some foxes."

The field were pressing hounds in spite of Laurence's appeals. Some children galloped over a field of seeds and several people were riding about on their own. We drew the last of Mr. Brooks' coverts, a long L-shaped plantation, blank.

"You can try Ashbury Wood or the common or Patchworth Copse now," said Mr. Brooks. "I don't think there's anywhere else. They're shooting on the Melcham side."

Kate looked frantically at Andrew and I knew she was thinking, not Ashbury Wood, nor the common.

"I think we'll try Patchworth Copse, sir," said Andrew.

The wind had dropped and for a moment a watery sun shone down on us.

Patchworth Copse was thick in undergrowth. There were large clumps of rhododendrons and privet, and acres of brambles and willow herb.

"Should be plenty of foxes here," said Andrew, sending Kate and me each to mark a ride. Laurence was keeping very close to hounds. A lot of people had gone home, but he still had Mr. Watson with him, and the Haywards and the Brooks and five or six other horsemen. Mr. Watson started to wade through the undergrowth, cracking his whip in the hope of putting up a fox.

I took a well-cut ride on the left of Andrew and rode on at a steady walk, keeping my eyes open for foxes.

It wasn't very long before hounds found. There was a crash of music, which became muffled as they hunted their fox into the rhododendrons. Soon they were hunting directly towards me and Daystar became frantic with impatience and I kept my eyes glued to the ride.

I saw the fox come across. He was a large, light-coloured fox, and because hounds were obviously hunting and because Andrew was very close, I didn't blow my whistle, but yelled: "Tally-ho over, tally-ho over." Andrew cheered hounds and they crossed the ride I was watching and hunted into some privet.

"Here, hold my horse," Andrew said a second later, throwing me Mulligatawny's reins and plunging into the privet on foot. I could hear the field galloping round outside the wood. Then I saw the fox come back across my ride and disappear into the rhododendrons again. I yelled to Andrew, and he put hounds on, and in a moment they were across the ride and back in the rhododendrons making the dickens of a row.

Andrew took Mulligatawny. "Try and stop him getting back next time, if you can," he told me. "Otherwise we'll be here all night."

But there wasn't a "next time," because the fox broke on the other side, across the ride, which Kate was watching, and then out into a ploughed field.

Mr. Brooks watched him cross the plough. Then he halloaed and halloaed and halloaed again. I joined the field, thundering down a ride after Laurence.

Andrew was just ahead, doubling the horn as hounds picked up the line again across the plough. Mr. Brooks wanted to catch another glimpse of the fox. He galloped on ahead and succeeded in heading him on the edge of a grass field; and very soon hounds were swinging left and hunting back towards Patchworth Copse again.

Andrew was furious. "Why can't Laurence keep him in order?" he muttered angrily. "He's spoilt the whole day. That fox will never leave the wood again; we'll be there until dark."

It had started to rain again: cold, sweeping rain which chilled us to the marrow of our bones.

Hounds hunted back into Patchworth Copse and then into the rhododendrons. I returned to the ride where I had first stood.

Nearly half an hour passed before the fox broke again; then he left the copse somewhere between me and Kate, across a field which was stubble. I heard Andrew blow the "gone-away." I gave Daystar her head and we galloped down the ride. The ground was treacherous: greasy on the surface and as hard as a bone underneath. We turned slowly at the bottom of the ride, but even then we nearly fell. The field was quite close. I could hear the dull thud of hoofs and the noise of branches scraping against hats, and blowing horses.

Hounds were hunting beautifully across the stubble. There was no sign of Andrew. I had expected to see him galloping on ahead with hounds. I hesitated for a moment. I wondered whether he was the wrong side of a wire fence; or had dismounted to encourage hounds through the privet and was now running back for his horse. Then I remembered that it is better for the first whipper-in to be with hounds than no one. I looked behind me and saw only the cold, dripping copse, before I sent Daystar into a gallop across the stubble and caught up with hounds as they checked at the edge of a spinney. I stood and watched them cast themselves, and hoped that Andrew would soon arrive and wondered where the field were, and Kate. Already I feared disaster. Then hounds hit "heelway"—that is, hunted the line the wrong way, back towards Patchworth Copse, instead of on towards Ashbury Wood—and for the next few minutes I was fully occupied stopping them. After that I cast them and they picked up the line again and hunted on towards Ashbury Wood. There was still no sign of Andrew, nor the field, nor Kate, and soon I fell to wishing that instead of casting hounds I had taken them back to Patchworth Copse. I foresaw myself losing them, and once more riding round and round Ashbury Wood and Letchworth Common. Besides, I doubted that I would ever be able to collect the pack together again without Andrew and without a horn.

Soon I had to take down several strands of wire before I could get through a fence. And by now, hounds were in Ashbury Wood and very near their fox, judging by the tone of their cry.

When I reached Ashbury Wood, hounds had stopped hunting. They came out one by one, first Gladsome, then Valiant, Vampire, True Love, Graceful, Dainty, Tempest. Gladsome's muzzle was covered with blood, so was Valiant's. I decided that they had killed their fox and I wished that Andrew was with me to share this moment of triumph. I looked across the field to Patchworth Copse, but I saw no gay flash of scarlet on the horizon; only a few cows toiling across distant fields to be milked, and, nearer, a crowd of chattering birds settling on a field of stubble.

I felt very helpless and hopelessly inadequate as I turned my attention to Ashbury Wood and wondered what to do next. If only someone would turn up, I thought, and I remembered the many occasions when I had scowled at Mr. Watson's approach or moved away because the field was coming. And now I was certain that some disaster had occurred of which I knew nothing.

Half the pack were standing around me. The rest were beginning to hunt rabbits in the wood. I decided to ride back.

I stood and called: "Come away back home, home. Come away back home, home, home." Only it didn't sound quite like that—the words ran into one another and home was long and echoed through the wood. More hounds appeared and they stopped hunting rabbits and my heart felt lighter, and I rode back across the field and took down the strands of wire again. Daystar was very quiet. She seemed to sense the responsibility we were sharing. The sky had an ominous look. Soon there would be more rain. I turned my coat collar up, and twisted the strands of wire round their post again and mounted, and then, suddenly, Daystar's head went up and I saw horsemen coming towards me—Laurence and Kate and the Haywards.

I counted hounds and found that I was one short, and again I called "Home, come away back home, home," before I galloped on towards the other horses.

Hounds came with me; behind me, in front of me and on each side of me. I suppose if I hadn't been worried about Andrew, it would have been one of the most wonderful moments of my life. Certainly I had achieved an ambition. How often I had dreamed of such a moment, when searching for lost hounds, or toiling after them while they cheerfully hunted rabbits. But now my thoughts were with Andrew, and I galloped towards the other horses with a heart filled with misgiving.

Kate and Laurence and the Haywards had halted their horses. They were watching me approach and suddenly I knew that they had decided to call it a day.

"What's happened? Where's Andrew?" I shouted when I was within earshot.

"Wait till you're nearer," yelled Laurence.

I reached them and drew rein. Now for the worst, I thought, seeing ambulances and stretchers and already visiting the South Bankley Hospital with *Horse and Hound* and flowers and chocolates in my hand. I missed Kate's first words.

"Turned too quickly," I heard her say. "He came quite a smack."

Then Laurence took up the narrative. "It's nothing

much," he said, looking at my alarmed face with a grin. "Andrew was galloping down one of those frightful rides. He turned a bit too sharply at the end and went for six. Somehow he knocked himself out and gave us all a terrible fright. As usual, Mr. Watson took control of the situation. In a jiffy he had loosened Andrew's hunting-tie—jolly silly thing to do actually, because he might have broken his neck for all he knew—and had given him buckets of cold tea out of his flask."

I could see it all in my mind's eye. I was glad I hadn't been there. I hate accidents.

It had started to rain. Hounds looked disconsolate.

"We managed to commandeer a car when he came to; or rather Mr. Watson did," Laurence continued, "and I rode to a call-box and rang up Mrs. Day. He looked quite cheerful going off in the car. Only he couldn't remember much."

"He's only concussed, I think," said Kate cheerfully. "We Days concuss far too easily. I've been concussed five times altogether."

"That accounts for a lot," said Laurence, grinning at me.

"Poor Andrew," I said. "He missed a kill, too. At least, I think they killed." And briefly I explained what had happened. Kate and Laurence were very pleased.

"We'll count it anyway," said Laurence.

"What a good thing you were there," said Kate. "Otherwise we might never have known."

"We'd better wend our way home," said Laurence. "Andrew will never rest till we're back. He was talking about the whereabouts of hounds all the time he was being supported to the car."

"I'm glad I wasn't there," I said.

The rain was beginning to come down in sheets.

"We're in for a wet night," said Laurence with a shiver. "Next season I'm going to wear scarlet. This wretched coat doesn't keep the rain out at all, and it's getting much too small."

"You mean you're getting much too big," said Kate.

"By the way, I've got the horn," said Laurence. "Andrew handed it to me through the window before he was driven away. I suppose we had better go back to Ashbury Wood and look for the missing hound, hadn't we? Do you know which it is?"

"No, I haven't worked it out yet," I answered.

"I bet it's Spendthrift," said Kate.

"If it is, he can jolly well find his own way home," said Laurence. "He's not worth the looking."

It took us ages to discover which hound was missing. First of all we thought it was Tomboy and then we saw him standing by himself under a tree, and Kate said we had lost Tell Tale and Laurence was certain it was Dainty. Spendthrift was very much in evidence, and finally we found that True Love was the missing hound, and, because he was young, we had no choice but to ride back to Ashbury Wood and search for him.

"Thank goodness we've got the horn, anyway," said Laurence, attempting to blow it, but only succeeding in making an awful gurgling noise.

The Haywards said "Good night," and disappeared in the rain in the direction of Melcham. Slowly the afternoon turned into evening. Our horn-blowing didn't sound at all professional. Kate said Laurence's efforts sounded like a cow trying to be sick, and Laurence said that Kate's sounded like a steamer's hooter on the Thames in August.

At last True Love appeared, wet and dismal, and we turned for home as a clock near Letchworth struck four.

"When did Valentine and Harry go home?" I asked, noticing, their absence for the first time.

"After the accident," said Laurence. "Someone had to take Mulligatawny home, and Harry was in an awful state anyway."

"One thing is, everything will be ready when we get back," said Kate. "I'm dying to get my wet clothes off."

We reached a road and a signpost which told us the way to Allate. The ditches were running with water. Soon it was dark, and we seemed alone in a blanket of rain—Kate and Laurence and myself, and our hunters and our hounds.

"This is the third thing," said Laurence, alluding to the theory that if you have one mishap you always have two more before things get better.

"Do you mean the rain or Andrew concussing himself?" asked Kate.

"Andrew, of course," said Laurence. "First you and Sandy got lost, then I did, and now Andrew's had a fall. It looks as though Valentine might get off this time."

"We simply must do well on Boxing Day," I said. "Our reputation must be mud by now."

"It's our last hope," said Kate. "Dad didn't think much of our last effort and he's coming out on Boxing Day."

"Thank goodness we killed today, anyway," said Laurence. "Mind you tell everyone, Kate."

Hounds were behaving beautifully. Laurence rode ahead. I was in the middle and Kate was behind. Cars came, and we saw glimmering headlights and heard a swish of water before they were lost again in the night. Bicyclists passed us, silent but for their tyres against the wet road, and once or twice we met people on foot wearing wellington boots and mackintoshes. "Thank goodness we didn't bring the terriers today," said Kate. "I bet they would have been tired by now."

We reached the top of the valley and the familiar path down.

"Oh for tea and a hot bath," sighed Kate.

"Oh for good news," said Laurence.

"I expect he's lying in a darkened room," said Kate. "I hope the doctor isn't a fussy one. Dr. Leighton's jolly sensible, but his assistants are awful. They always try and make you stay in bed, even when you've only got a temperature of 37.5 centigrade. They'll probably say he's to stay in bed for a week and then we've had it, because Boxing Day's on Monday."

Laurence and I hadn't thought of Boxing Day being on Monday, nor of Andrew being kept in bed. We were struck dumb with horror.

"But that would be terrible," said Laurence at last. "We've advertised the meet. Half the county's coming. Oh, gosh, what can we do?"

"Don't let's jump our fences before we come to them," said Kate. "If I know Andrew, it'll take more than a doctor to keep him in bed."

Laurence was seeing Chidlington Market Place,

crowds of people and no hounds. "We'll have to go to the meet anyway," he said.

Long Chill Farm sent a faint glimmer of light across the valley. It looked like a ship alone in a sea of rain. Bert Saunders was waiting for us in the kennel-yard. He had a sack across his shoulders to protect him from the rain. He told us the doctor had been and had spent a long time with Andrew, and that he thought Andrew must be pretty bad and that Valentine was that upset. Kate looked frightened and Laurence murmured "Boxing Day." I recalled past stories Bert Saunders had told me. I knew he revelled in catastrophe. I said "Don't worry," to Kate. "He always exaggerates." Kate wanted to give a view-halloa so that Valentine or Harry would come out and tell us the latest news; but Laurence stopped her. He said that she would wake Andrew and that Valentine was probably busy, or in her bath. The horses were very wet. We put Overture and Daystar into spare boxes and rubbed them down and put straw under their rugs.

Then we helped Kate and Bert Saunders dry hounds, and look them over for cuts and thorns, and feed them. Then at last we ran indoors, awkwardly, because our legs were stiff from being wet so long, and met Mrs. Day in the kitchen and heard the latest news.

Andrew, she told us, was only concussed. He was at present asleep in bed and would have to stay there for at least two days; after which he would have to keep quiet and not ride or do anything exciting for another three.

"But that's five whole days," cried Kate.

"And it's Boxing Day on Monday," wailed Laurence.

"Well, it's no good complaining," said Mrs. Day briskly. "That's what Dr. Leighton said, and you know he's not fussy."

"It's tragic," wailed Kate. "What are we going to do?"

"If you make so much noise you'll waken Andrew," said Mrs. Day. "And then he'll take even longer to get better. If he starts having headaches, he's to return to bed immediately. Dr. Leighton said that he should take it easy for a fortnight first of all; only Andrew made such a fuss he relented and said that five days to a week would do. But he's absolutely forbidden him to hunt on Boxing Day."

"Hallo," said Valentine, coming into the kitchen. "I didn't know you were back. Why didn't you shriek? I meant to help settle the horses and feed hounds. Isn't it awful about Andrew?"

"Tragic," cried Kate.

"What on earth are we going to do about Boxing Day?" asked Laurence.

"Andrew says Sandy's to hunt hounds," said Valentine. "He's quite firm about it."

"Me?" I cried in horror, staring at Valentine. "But I couldn't possibly. I don't know the first thing about it."

I tried to see myself putting hounds into covert, taking them out, blowing the "gone-away." I had often dreamed of myself hunting hounds. Ever since the beginning of the Chill Valley Foxhounds it had been the greatest of my ambitions. But I hadn't expected to hunt hounds this year, nor next year. Always such a moment had belonged to the rather distant future.

"He's right, of course," I heard Kate say, and I realised that I was standing with my mouth open while the others talked.

"I couldn't possibly," I said weakly, looking across the Days' kitchen to where the chipped blue-and-white mugs hung on the cream-coloured dresser.

"It would be the end of the Chill Valley Hunt. No one would ever come out again."

"Defeatist," said Valentine.

"*Nothing venture, nothing win,*" quoted Kate.

"If Andrew says you can hunt hounds, you can," said Laurence, sounding uncertain of the fact himself.

"But I can't even blow the 'gone-away' properly," I objected.

"Well, you've got till Monday to practise," said Valentine. "You can take the horn home with you to-night and blow it all to-morrow, and the next day and the day after that."

"In fact, every day until Monday," said Kate.

"What about our parents?" asked Laurence. "They'll have nervous breakdowns and throw us out of house and home."

"You'll have to blow it outside then," said Valentine. "Go for long walks with Quinky and practise."

"I'll have to practise making hunting noises too," I said. "I shall be hopeless at putting hounds into covert. I can't make the right noises at all."

"Pity we haven't got those hunting records you can buy," said Laurence.

"There's no sense in making a toil out of a pleasure," said Mrs. Day. "If it's going to worry you, I should call the do off."

"But we couldn't possibly," cried Kate, sounding horrified.

"We've advertised the meet," Laurence told her. "The whole county's coming."

"Well, why not just hold the meet and then ride home again?" suggested Mrs. Day helpfully.

"That would never do," said Laurence firmly. "We can't afford to offend our subscribers."

"I shall pray for a hard frost," I said. "Honestly, I can't possibly hunt hounds. I'm quite incompetent."

"Nonsense," said Valentine. "Your hunting noises sound jolly professional sometimes."

"Yes, *sometimes*," I said.

"And you can blow the horn better than any of us, except for Andrew," she continued.

"You two had better go home," said Mrs. Day, looking at Laurence's and my wet clothes. "You'll catch your deaths of cold hanging about in those wet things."

"Can't we see Andrew before we go?" I asked.

"I don't think you had better," said Mrs. Day. "Come and see him in the morning when he's feeling better. He's asleep now and I do want him to get a good night's rest."

"He keeps talking about hunting," said Valentine.

"Buck up and get home," said Mrs. Day, taking Laurence by the shoulders and steering him towards the back door. "You'll both get pneumonia hanging about, and then what will your mother say? And you, Kate, go and have your bath."

"I'll help them off first," said Kate.

"No, you won't," said Mrs. Day.

"I will," said Valentine, opening the back door and looking out. At last it had stopped raining. The night was pitch-black. The horses were tired and we led them along the familiar rutty track now running with water. Little Hall's lights shone bravely across the valley. I felt tired, too tired to worry any more about the meet on Boxing Day. It may snow or freeze before then, I told myself, and turned my thoughts to Christmas and to spring, and the months beyond.

TEN

I wakened at dawn on Thursday. All night I had dreamed of hunting hounds. It was too early to telephone the Days and ask after Andrew. Outside, it was still dark, but for a narrow strip of grey in the east. To sleep again was impossible; my head was whirling with thoughts of Boxing Day. I rose and dressed, and, collecting Andrew's horn and Quinky, I went out into the early morning.

I walked down into the valley and met a thick, damp fog. The hedges and trees were dripping. Otherwise all the land seemed still. For a moment, I couldn't bear to break the silence. Then I raised the horn to my lips and blew "all on," and "cope forrard," and "across the ride," and the toots Andrew blows when he's drawing a covert. And finally, in a fit of optimism, I blew the "gone-away," and "the kill," and "gone to ground." But, though I blew them, not one of my efforts sounded in the least professional. Only "all on," and "cope forrard," were passably good. Quinky went home and I felt like "a phantom huntsman" or a strange ghost, alone in the midst of the fog. The grey light of dawn brightened and I continued to practise blowing the horn until my mouth felt dry and my throat ached. Then my thoughts turned to breakfast, and suddenly I discovered that I was lost in our own familiar valley.

If you've been lost, and I expect you have, you'll know how I felt after I had walked twice in a circle and arrived back each time at the same piece of ploughed field. It seemed particularly stupid to be lost somewhere so near home. I decided that in future I would carry a compass, and I wished that I was like the huntsman of the Path Hill Foxhounds, who, according to Andrew, carries one in his head. My watch told me that the time was eight o'clock. I thought of the alarm clock ringing in the passage at home and my parents expecting me to answer it.

I blew the horn again, but my efforts, instead of improving, seemed to be steadily deteriorating. I felt disheartened. I decided to tell Andrew that I couldn't possibly hunt hounds on Boxing Day. Then, quite suddenly, the fog lifted, revealing a sky peculiarly blue for December, and the chimney stacks of Long Chill Farm house.

I was surprised. I had imagined I was far nearer home. I wondered whether my horn-blowing efforts had wakened Andrew. I guessed that Valentine and Kate would probably be already in the kennels. I summoned my remaining energy and ran across the plough towards Long Chill Farm.

Mrs. Day was cooking breakfast in the kitchen.

"Andrew's still asleep," she told me.

I borrowed the Days' telephone and rang up Laurence.

He had heard my horn blowing efforts in the valley. He said that they had sounded quite all right and that he would feed the horses and join me later.

As I had guessed, Kate and Valentine were busy in the kennels. I joined them and helped wash down the courts and lodging-rooms. Later, we all had breakfast in the Day's big farmhouse kitchen—porridge, two fried eggs and rashers of home-cured bacon, followed by toast or bread and dairy butter, and honey or marmalade or home-made raspberry jam; and, of course, coffee, or tea if you preferred it.

After I had helped wash up, I visited Andrew, who looked pale, but otherwise more or less as usual.

I asked him whether he really wanted me to hunt hounds, and suggested that it might be better to cancel the meet on Boxing Day, or at least go and then come back. Andrew looked at me and grinned. "You've got to begin some time, Sandy," he said. "You already know far more than I did when I started."

"I doubt it. Anyway, you're far quicker in the uptake than me," I said. "I'm incredibly slow-witted."

"I've noticed it," said Andrew, grinning and sounding sarcastic.

I wished Andrew wouldn't treat Boxing Day as a joke. He seemed to find the fact that I would have to hunt hounds extremely funny.

"What about our reputation?" I asked. "We don't want it to sink any lower."

"It can't. It's too low already," said Andrew. "It's reached rock-bottom. Anyway, it's not as though I hunt hounds so dashed well. You may easily prove to be the better huntsman."

I gave a cry of horror. "Not likely," I said. "I can't even blow the horn properly, much less make the right noises at the right time."

"You can blow the horn all right," said Andrew, "if that was you practising at some unearthly hour this morning."

"Yes, it was me," I admitted. "Don't say I woke you up?"

"No, I was already awake when I heard you," said Andrew. "You really did sound quite professional. For a moment I thought it was Sam Wells or some other diehard huntsman come back to life."

I felt heartened. Andrew generally means what he says. I suddenly felt much happier about Boxing Day. Perhaps, after all, I would succeed in hunting hounds reasonably well. I imagined the wind in my face, and saw the hilly country around Hettington in my mind's eye.

Then I thought of the meet and the crowd of onlookers in the market place. I saw myself looking absurdly young in my black coat and crash-cap, with a horn between my coat buttons, and beneath it all a heart as heavy as lead.

"I shall look awfully silly hunting hounds in a black coat," I said. "Surely I ought to have a scarlet collar, or at least coloured revers?"

"Yes, of course you should," said Andrew, sitting up in bed. "I had forgotten all about it. You can't possibly hunt hounds in your ordinary coat. What are we going to do?"

"Hallo," said Laurence, coming into the room. "Your Mum said I would find you both up here."

"What are we going to do, Laurence?" cried Andrew. "Sandy's only got a black coat, and she must have something special if she's going to hunt hounds."

"Gosh, why didn't we think of it before?" asked Laurence.

"But we didn't know I was to hunt hounds until last night," I said.

"Was that when it all happened? Only yesterday?" asked Andrew. "It seems years and years since that dreadful meet at Little Bottom Farm."

"Look, I think you had better rest a bit more," said Laurence, looking upset. "We're worrying you."

"Did Mulligatawny slip? Is that why he came down? And who supported me to the car? Don't be silly," said Andrew, as Laurence started to back towards the door. "It can't hurt me to know what happened."

"Oh, all right," said Laurence, sitting down on the bottom of Andrew's bed. "I'll tell you the whole story and after that you must go to sleep. Else you'll never get better."

"All right, nurse," said Andrew, grinning.

Laurence related the events of yesterday from the moment Andrew put hounds into Patchworth Copse, until when we arrived back at kennels tired and wet.

When he had finished, Andrew said: "It's so annoying that it should happen like that. Just cantering down a ride. It shows you shouldn't be cautious, because if something's coming to you, it comes whatever happens. I wish I had concussed myself jumping a brook or racing hounds to a railway line. It would have been much more dashing."

"Still, you might have made other people nervous if

you had," said Laurence. "But no one's likely to stop coming out hunting because you concussed yourself cantering down a ride."

"What did the field think?" asked Andrew.

"They were horribly upset," said Laurence. "Especially poor Mr. Watson. He got himself in quite a state. Mr. Austin-Smith stayed the calmest. I thought Mrs. Simmons would never stop talking."

"You'll have to redeem our name on Boxing Day," said Andrew, grinning at me. "It's our last hope."

"We're lost, then," I said, looking out of the window and wishing I was one of those people who are not afraid of anything and that I was cocksure and competent and quick-witted and, most important of all, capable of hunting hounds.

"You know, I believe we've got some scarlet material which would do for Sandy's coat in one of the chests," Andrew told Laurence. "Could you ask Mum about it? I believe it's in the bottom of the chest in the hall."

"But that's wonderful," said Laurence.

We talked for a little longer before we bade Andrew farewell and Laurence told him to go to sleep, and I told him to make a startling recovery, so that he could hunt hounds after all on Boxing Day. Then we rushed downstairs and found Mrs. Day, who was most obliging and soon produced nearly a yard of scarlet material.

"Bring your coat back after lunch," she told me, "and I'll sew it on the collar and then you'll be all right for Boxing Day."

"Yes, come on, we must go," said Laurence. "We haven't groomed our horses yet and it's nearly eleven o'clock."

I thanked Mrs. Day for her kind offer and promised to bring my coat back later in the day.

Thursday and Friday passed all too quickly. Christmas Eve came with a south-west wind and a cloudy sky, and a forecast which promised warm days ahead.

The thought of Boxing Day lay heavy on my mind. Even the frantic last-minute rush of Christmas shopping failed to dispel it. I became absent-minded and maddened my family. I labelled Mummy's present—a pair of evening gloves—"Laurence, with best wishes from Sandy," and Laurence's present—a sporting print—"Mummy, with love from Sandy." I gave Daystar two teas on Friday and forgot to give her any breakfast on Saturday. I let the iron burn the ironing-blanket, and didn't notice when a saucepan of onion soup boiled over on our Aga stove, which I was actually leaning against at the time.

I continued to practise blowing the horn and forced Laurence out into the valley to listen to me and criticise.

Mr. Austin-Smith telephoned the Days and asked when we wanted Lost Horizon. Valentine answered and persuaded him to keep her until after Boxing Day. The weather-cock stayed firmly pointing to the south-west.

Laurence, Kate and I took hounds out on Christmas Eve. We gave them nearly two hours' slow exercise, and, except for losing Spendthrift immediately after leaving the kennels and Rattler upsetting a dustbin and Tomboy visiting someone's kitchen, our pack behaved beautifully. Needless to say we had left the puppies at home. We took them out later on foot.

On the evening of Christmas Eve, because Boxing

Day seemed so desperately close and it seemed certain that I should have to hunt hounds, I tried to think only of Christmas.

I washed my breeches and wondered whether my aunts would send the usual five pound notes, and whether Father Christmas would come again and hoped Mummy would like her gloves and Daddy his carefully chosen, expensive handkerchiefs. I thought about Daystar while I cleaned my boots. I decided that I would enter her for some hunter trials in the spring, and that I must try and school her more often during the summer, and that she would have to have her annual holiday in May. While I ironed my white hunting-shirt, I thought about Lost Horizon and Mr. Austin-Smith's astounding generosity. But all the time in the back of my mind there was Boxing Day. It was more to me than Christmas, or Daystar's future, or Lost Horizon's possibilities. Ever since that fateful Wednesday I had dreamed of hunting hounds each night, and each morning, as I opened my eyes, my thoughts had been of Boxing Day.

Andrew was allowed to get up on Christmas Eve, but he wasn't allowed to coach me in the art of blowing a horn, nor could he ride or go outside the house for more than a few minutes.

The Mayor of Hettington telephoned Laurence and told him that he and some fellow-aldermen and councillors were arranging a reception for us on the steps of the Town Hall on Boxing Day. Laurence was horrified. He had known it would be a large meet, but now it would be a smart one as well. He told the Mayor about Andrew being concussed and about the youthful first whipper-in who would be hunting hounds for the first time. Apparently the Mayor was very jovial and said: "All the better. A new broom sweeps clean." Then he told Laurence that he was a keen amateur photographer and hoped to take a film of the meet and of us drawing our first covert.

"So now all our mistakes are to be recorded," said Laurence bitterly, after he had finished talking to the Mayor and replaced the receiver. "They will be immortal. Perhaps even future generations will learn how not to hunt from our mistakes."

Poor Laurence had less faith than anyone in my ability to hunt hounds. I suppose he knew all my failings too well, besides being pessimistic by nature. Kate, always an escapist, refused to think about Boxing Day. When I asked her on Christmas Eve whether she honestly thought I should be able to hunt hounds when the moment came, she was evasive.

"I don't see why you shouldn't," she said, "and for goodness' sake don't let's make a toil out of a pleasure."

Valentine gave me a great deal of advice. "Keep calm," she told me a dozen times. "Then you'll be all right. And remember it's better to help hounds too little than to be forever interfering; and don't think about the field or of anything but hunting."

Andrew was tiresomely cheerful. "What does it matter?" he said, when I moaned about my incompetence. "You'll only be living up to our reputation for madness, if you do lose hounds in the first covert, or blow mad notes on the horn, or fall off, or run away, or do whatever you think you're going to do."

But Mummy and Daddy were definitely pleased to

think that I should be hunting hounds on Boxing Day. They were determined to attend the meet and threatened to follow me to the first covert in the car. Gladys and Mr. Mitchell were delighted, too. They were certain that I should have my photograph in the morning papers. Gladys helped me starch my hunting-tie and Mr. Mitchell offered to come early on Boxing Day so that he could help us get our hunters ready.

And so Christmas came, warm and wet, and the weathercock told us that the wind was still in the south-west, and all around people grumbled because it wasn't a white Christmas; except in Long Chill Farm House, where the Days celebrated the weather by opening an extra bottle of wine.

Laurence and I had a wonderful Christmas. My parents gave me a sandwich case to take hunting, which was something I had been wanting for ages, and Laurence gave me a book on horn-blowing and a new tail bandage for Daystar. The Days had all joined together and they presented Laurence and me with a marvellous picture called "A Foxhunter's Dream." Then I had lots of useful presents like money from my aunts, bath salts from Gladys and a fountain-pen from Quinky. Father Christmas came as usual and filled one of my socks with dozens of things I couldn't do without any longer—an iodine pencil to take hunting, safety-pins, a Puffin book called *Riding for Children* by Henry Wynmalen, a handkerchief, chocolate, and, of course, at the bottom, the traditional tangerine.

In the evening we had the usual Christmas dinner and afterwards Laurence and I washed up, because we wouldn't be there to do it the next day.

We had visited Long Chill Farm during the morning, and had helped Valentine, Kate and Harry mix a special Christmas pudding for hounds. We had also presented the Days with their Christmas presents and tasted their home-made wine and looked at the horses and discussed the morrow.

I had been at school when Andrew and Laurence had looked at the land we were to hunt on Boxing Day. Now they made a map for me to study, with the coverts to be drawn marked in red, and gates and jumpable fences marked in blue. They also drew a weathercock in one corner. I looked at it in bed on Christmas night. Andrew had told me which way each covert should be drawn if the wind was still in the south-west. I tried to memorise it all: to carry the map in my head, like the huntsman of the Path Hill carries his compass. It was after twelve when at last I turned off the light and fell asleep to dream, not of hunting, as I had expected, but of chasing thieves round and round Hettington before finally running them to earth in the Town Hall, where the Mayor was waiting to present me with a gold medal for my courage.

I wakened with a start. I knew that before me was a day fraught with difficulties, but for a moment I couldn't remember what was at stake. Then it all came to me and I threw myself out of bed, thinking that I would give anything to stay in bed and spend Boxing Day at home. The alarm clock was ringing, and already in my mind's eye I could see crowds and Hettington Market Place. I wished that I was anywhere but at home with the prospect of hunting hounds in front of me.

I wakened Laurence and dressed.

Daystar and Overture were dirtier than usual, because we hadn't done much to them on Christmas Day. I had to wash Daystar's tail, her head and a large part of her quarters. Later, I plaited her mane and strapped her with a body-brush, and oiled her hoofs and gave her a last polish with a rubber.

I took ages dressing. Mrs. Day had made a very good job of my coat. The scarlet on the collar looked as though it had always been there. Andrew had said that if it was a success Kate must have scarlet on her coat, too, then everyone would know we were hunt servants. I decided that it *was* a success and that I looked much smarter than usual, and more grown up.

I said good-bye to my parents and Gladys and Mr. Mitchell, who had both come to wish me luck. I told them not to be optimistic and that I should probably lose hounds before we even reached Hettington.

Mummy said: "Don't be silly. I'm sure you'll manage beautifully. You must know nearly as much as Andrew by now and you always seem to be there."

"Oh, I'm not!" I cried. "I'm always getting lost. And as for knowing as much as Andrew——"

"Of course you'll be all right," said Daddy. "And, anyway, if you're not, it won't alter the fate of nations, and the sun will rise to-morrow just the same."

Laurence and I mounted our horses, and Gladys said: "Have you remembered your sandwiches?" I looked at the new case hanging from my saddle and wondered whether I should feel like, or have time to eat, the turkey sandwiches inside.

Laurence said: "Yes, thank you. They look lovely."

Mr. Mitchell said: "Mind you kill a fox. I want to see one of you coming home with a mask hanging from the saddle."

Mummy said: "Be careful."

Daddy said: "See you at the meet if the car starts."

Then Laurence and I rode out into the warm December morning; down into the valley, grey and brown and beautiful to us with that friendly, lasting beauty which comes when you've known a place for a long time, when each tree and hedge, each rise in the ground, each track or stile or gate or fence brings a past incident to mind.

The sky was grey, and, beneath the horses' hoofs, the track was wet. There was a breeze in the air, and in the distance we could see that the branches of Allate's trees were nodding.

Laurence and I were silent. I think each of our minds held the same thoughts. I had two pictures in front of me. In one, hounds were running and near them was myself leaning forward and blowing a perfect "gone-away," while in front stretched a long succession of hedges, and behind an enthusiastic field galloped on large horses, crying to each other: "By jove, can't she hunt!"

The other picture was quite different. In it there was rain and a cold bleak covert and a miserable grumbling field. There were hounds hunting rabbits, and me muddy and disreputable, blowing a horn which wouldn't blow. Everything told of failure, and when that picture appeared I hastened to forget it and substitute the other.

Valentine, Kate, Harry and Mr. Day were waiting for us by the kennel-yard. They waved as we approached, and Andrew came out of the house wearing an overcoat.

"Wonderful morning for scent," called Mr. Day.

"Did you sleep?" asked Kate. Andrew looked miserable and unfamiliar in his overcoat and a thick muffler.

"I wish I could come," he said. "It's the sort of morning I've always dreamed about. Oh, I'm so sick of being treated like an invalid. I felt like breaking a window or throwing something at someone last night. If it hadn't been Christmas Day I think I would have. I rang up Dr. Leighton this morning. I thought he might be in a good mood and relent, and say I could hunt today. But no such luck."

"Andrew's been terrible," said Valentine.

"Hadn't we better go?" asked Kate. "It's gone nine."

"Are you coming in the car?" Laurence asked Andrew.

"No, I couldn't bear it," Andrew answered. "Anyway, I'm not supposed to drive until the day after tomorrow."

Kate opened the draw-yard gate and the yard was suddenly full of hounds.

I called "Cope forrard," and made the sort of noises I've heard Andrew make, when we leave the kennels on a hunting morning. Mrs. Day called: "Have a good time and good luck." Andrew looked at me and said: "Keep calm. Remember to blow hounds out of a covert when you've drawn it blank; otherwise you'll hear something from Laurence and the field. Draw the coverts up-wind; look out for hounds hitting heelway; and don't turn imbecile because you've made a few mistakes."

"Okay," I said, wondering how Andrew expected me to remember so many instructions. "But don't expect anything but incompetence."

"All on," said Kate. "For goodness" sake get moving, Sandy, before I lose half of them."

"Good-bye," said Andrew. "Mind you kill a brace. You all look very smart."

We rode away down the lane. Hounds gambolled ahead of me. Valentine was acting as first whipper-in. She rode in front. We had left the terriers at home. I refused to think of the next few hours. Daystar was fresh. She wanted to be in front. The breeze was blowing in my face. I felt the horn between my coat buttons. "Your great moment has come, Sandy Dashwood," I thought. "To-day you carry the horn."

ELEVEN

I don't know how we ever reached Hettington.

We discovered that Spendthrift was missing soon after we left Allate, and after a frantic search he was eventually found in the village bakery. Meanwhile, Conscript and Ludlow had vanished, and, in spite of my amateurish efforts on the horn, they didn't return, until Valentine found them in a rubbish-dump, already well known to myself and Kate, and drove them back to where the rest of us were waiting on the road.

Hettington Market Place was seething with people. My heart fell when I saw them and I had an awful sinking feeling in the pit of my stomach. Policemen cleared a path for us to the Town Hall, Kate and Valentine kept hounds together, and, somehow, we reached the steps and were greeted by the Mayor and his aldermen and councillors. For an awful moment I thought the Mayor was about to deliver a speech. I imagined remarks about teenagers and kindergarten huntsmen and "this unique pack." Then the Mayor shook me by the hand and said how pleased he was to see us here today.

I don't think I shall ever forget the meet. There were so many people and so many cameras, and so many prams which hounds were determined to look inside.

Kate hadn't a chance to keep hounds together. They just vanished between people's legs and reappeared in the Town Hall, or, like Spendthrift, were later seen trotting down Friar Street.

I had an embarrassing time. Members of the field approached me and pressed pound coins into my hands, muttering: "For you and the whips," or, "For the good of the hunt," or just "Happy New Year."

By the time the hands of the clock on the Town Hall had reached eleven-fifteen I had nearly twenty-eight pounds in my pocket. As you can imagine, I felt an awful fraud, though, for the sake of the hunt, I was delighted to have so much money handed to me. The Mayor gave us all cherry brandy, even Harry, who thus achieved a lifelong ambition.

At twenty past eleven Laurence gave the order to move off. Valentine and Kate tried to collect hounds and I blew the horn, much to my amazement, and rode out of the Market Place, while all around cameras clicked.

Laurence directed me to the first covert. It was a long, narrow fir plantation and beyond it lay a farm and hills. I seemed to have quite a lot of hounds. Valentine was still with me; she said that Kate was pursuing Conscript and Spendthrift round the back streets of Hettington. I sent Valentine to watch the far corner of the plantation on the down-wind side. Then I put hounds in.

Laurence had halted the field, which looked enormous

and was unusually loud-voiced. I rode into the plantation, which hadn't much undergrowth and which I didn't think would hold a fox. I wondered how much noise to make. I wanted to keep the field informed of my whereabouts; but the plantation wasn't very large, so I guessed Laurence would be able to keep me in view quite easily. I blew a toot on the horn. I called: "Y-i-t tra high. Push 'em up there." Then, as Tell Tale spoke: "Hike, hike, hike to Tell Tale, hike."

But Tell Tale was only hunting rabbits, and a minute later, I was rating him, not too loudly, because I didn't want the field to hear. Soon I was blowing hounds out.

"You didn't see anything, did you?" I asked Valentine.

"No, nothing except a rabbit," she answered. "Kate's appeared again. She's sending hounds on behind. Shall I come on with you?"

"Okay," I answered, riding towards a coppice beyond the farm. Valentine counted hounds. "They're all on," she said. I blew three short notes on the horn to tell Kate to come forward. I heard a thunder of hoofs as the field caught up with us.

"Where are you heading for?" asked Laurence, riding alongside.

I pointed to the coppice. "Is that okay?" I asked.

"Yes, quite," said Laurence. "It's got a fair bit of undergrowth and a pit with an earth in it, which the farmer promised to stop."

I felt very cheerful as I rode with hounds on each side of me, behind and in front. Valentine galloped to the farthest corner of the coppice. Kate stayed with me until we were past the farm, then she, too, went on.

The wind was still in the south-west. I chanted: "*A*

south-west wind and a cloudy sky makes the scent lie breast-high." I felt like Will Ogilvie's *Happiest Man in England* who "*would not change his place with kings.*" All my fears had vanished. I felt madly cheerful and suddenly certain of a good day, as I rode towards the brown and green coppice beyond the farm.

There were several people standing on a hilltop in the distance. I thought I could distinguish Mr. Watson, and, to my horror, my parents and Quinky. I put hounds into the coppice. "Leu in, leu in there. Elu there, little ladies. Ki try for him," I called as the pack surged into the undergrowth beneath the trees. I jumped a stile, and, as I landed in the wood, Gladsome spoke. "This is it," I thought, knowing that Gladsome could be trusted. "Try for him, try," I cried, and then, as Gladsome spoke again: "Hike to Gladsome, hike, hike."

I felt terribly excited and now Rattler and Vampire and Valiant were speaking, too; another moment and nearly the whole pack were on the line of a fox. They hunted through bracken into rhododendrons and then for a minute they were silent. I halted Daystar and watched and waited, but not for long; soon Vampire was speaking again, his deep notes echoing through the wood.

"Hike to Vampire," I cried, hoping I wasn't making too much noise. "Hike, hike, hike."

All the pack were together hunting furiously through the undergrowth. Soon they were making a tremendous noise. Then, suddenly, they were silent. He must have broken, I thought, or else he's gone to ground. I stood still while hounds feathered along a ride. Daystar was trembling with excitement. Then I heard a whistle loud and clear. I doubled the horn. Someone halloaed. I gave Daystar her head and we galloped through the wood. It took me a moment to find Kate. She was standing near a few acres of kale holding her hat in the air. She waved frantically when she saw me, and yelled: "He's a big, dark fox. He entered the kale just about here." Hounds had already picked up the line. They were hunting directly towards Kate.

I shouted: "Cop—forrard—aw—ay." In the wood Valentine was sending Spendthrift on. The field came into sight. There were dozens of large horses as well as a multitude of ponies.

By now hounds had reached the kale. True Love and Gladsome were well to the fore. Kate was already watching the far corner. Very soon a fox came out, a large, dark fox, which we could all see from where we stood. I resisted the temptation to lift hounds out of the kale and take them on to where the fox was now slipping through a hedge into a ploughed field.

I let them hunt the line through the kale and then to the hedge and on to the plough beyond. Once, for a moment, they checked, and then they were away again, running uphill to where Mr. Watson and Mummy and Daddy were enjoying a wonderful view. I rode Daystar at the hedge, and, as we landed, I saw a gaping ditch and a murderous strand of wire. I thanked Providence for a horse which jumps with scope, before I turned and yelled: "Wire, 'ware wire." I saw Valentine turn away. But I was too late to stop Kate. She came over, landing well into the next field.

"Isn't this wonderful?" she cried. "Aren't hounds hunting beautifully?"

"Don't speak too soon," I said, watching hounds swing right-handed half-way up the hill, and thinking that Kate should be ahead on the down-wind of the pack instead of with me.

We had reached the hill by now and I sent Kate along the bottom, so that she would see the fox if he turned and started running back towards the coppice. A second later I saw Mr. Watson waving his cap and knew that the fox had gone over the brow of the hill. I blew "Cope forrard," for Kate's benefit and then I leaned well forward, and let Daystar's long strides carry me up the hill.

Down on the other side of the hill there was a new world. Rich farmland lay before us, acres and acres of it, and, in the distance, grey factory chimneys and gasworks stood out against the grey sky.

The field had found a way round the hedge with the wire, and as I started to gallop down towards the valley I could hear their hoofs pounding up the hill. Vampire was a little behind and Spendthrift still hadn't come on; otherwise the pack were together, hunting beautifully. They checked for a moment at the bottom of the hill on the edge of some plough, and the field caught up and Laurence rode forward, and said: "Well done, Sandy. They're hunting magnificently."

Then Charmer picked up the line again, and we were running once more.

Beyond the plough were Jersey cows and a straggling wired hedge with rails in one corner, towards which I turned. Hounds checked near the cows, but only for a few seconds, then they were running like smoke towards a distant spinney. I jumped the rails and felt Daystar scrape the top. I looked back and saw that the field was already smaller and guessed that some of its members were still on the wrong side of the hedge. Daystar was going well. She felt fit, and ready to gallop for hours and hours. In front was a wire fence, but in the middle of it there was a water-trough with a rail above. I remembered Andrew's stories about the huntsman of the Path Hill—he had always jumped water-troughs if that was the only way round a wire fence. I looked for a gate and saw one far away in a distant corner. I turned towards the trough, hoping that the take-off wasn't too poached, and used my legs as I felt Daystar hesitate. The next moment we were over and bearing down on a farmyard where a man stood waving his cap. "'E's 'eading for the spinney," he shouted, as I drew near. "Can't be much more than thirty seconds ahead of them."

I waved my thanks and galloped on. I wondered whether hounds would kill their fox when he reached the spinney. I half hoped they wouldn't, because I doubted that I could cut off the mask and hang it on Laurence's or my saddle. And yet I knew it would do our pack a great deal of good to kill their fox, not to mention our reputation.

But I was not left long in doubt. Hounds checked in the spinney and it was several minutes before they picked up the line again.

I watched hounds cast themselves while the field dismounted, loosened their girths, smoked and ate sandwiches, took swigs from their flasks, and, of course, talked.

Daystar was glad of the rest, and, while hounds

feathered round the spinney, I took stock of the landscape and made up my mind where the fox had gone. In front of us was a field, which I guessed by its appearance had recently been grazed by sheep. Beyond it were several grass fields, in one of which there was an acre or more of gorse, where I suspected there would be an earth. I decided that the smell of sheep had killed the line across the next field, but that if I took hounds on to the next hedge they would pick up the line and hunt to the gorse, where I thought our fox might have gone to ground. Of course I knew I might be wrong. The fox might have doubled back towards the first covert or turned left and be heading for the osier beds down by the river. There were plenty of possibilities. But no more than most huntsmen have to contend with. I blew a toot on the horn and hounds swung in my direction with one accord. If only my guess is correct, I thought, hardly daring to hope for so much as I galloped on towards the hedge.

I needn't have worried. Providence, fate, luck, all seemed with me. Hounds were hunting again before they reached the hedge; hunting all together towards the gorse three fields away.

I jumped the hedge and took down some wire, and opened a gate and reached the gorse, just in time to see hounds leaving it.

Kate had caught up with me while I was undoing the wire. She was now on my left on the down-wind side of hounds. Valentine was just behind me and in front of the field. Evening was already in the air. Soon there would be a mist coming up from the river meadows. Already the outlines of the distant factory chimneys and the gasworks were blurred. I looked at my watch and saw that it was half-past three. Hours and hours seemed to have passed since the meet in Hettington Market Place. It might have been yesterday or the day before or even a week ago. Daystar was beginning to tire a little. In front was more plough, and, beyond it, a field of kale through which hounds were already hunting. I chose a furrow and leaned well forward as we crossed the plough. I rode over a bank and the next moment I was watching hounds in the kale.

Vampire was working well. As I watched him, I knew why Andrew said he was worth two of the other hounds.

Valentine arrived and galloped on to watch a corner of the kale. The field came over the bank: first Laurence, then a man wearing scarlet and a topper, then the Haywards and several people in ratcatcher, and Roger Wilcox, and, a little later, Harry and several other small sporting children on moorland ponies. They all halted a few yards from the kale and patted their steaming hunters and discussed the run.

Meanwhile hounds were hustling their tired fox round the kale. I saw him several times as I rode backwards and forwards cracking my whip. In the distance I could see Mr. Watson coming towards us. The kale was very wet and soon my breeches and boots were soaking.

Then I saw Valentine raise her cap and blow her whistle; and everyone could see the fox as he loped away from the kale towards a small, grey farm in the distance.

Another moment and hounds were out of the kale and running faster than ever. I think everyone thought they would bowl him over, but somehow he dodged them all and reached a copse, and here hounds checked again.

I guessed our fox had gone to ground. I gave Valentine Daystar's reins and plunged into the copse, which was thick in undergrowth. I found an earth quite quickly. Some obliging person had stopped it with a bundle of faggots. I wondered whether that was due to Andrew's and Laurence's reconnaissance work before Christmas, or whether it was just a kind thought from a pro-hunting farmer.

Hounds were working well. I started to wade back through the undergrowth. Then I heard Kate's whistle and I was seized by panic. I tried to run, and, catching my foot in brambles, I fell headlong. I picked myself up and rushed on, scratching my face and hands. I thought of hounds running and myself still on foot in the copse. But just when I was becoming really frantic I saw light through the trees and Valentine waiting.

"He's broken the far side," she yelled.

At the same moment hounds picked up the line again. There was a wild, heart-stirring crash of music.

I could hear Kate crying: "Forrard away, forrard away." I fumbled with my stirrups. Daystar was whirling her quarters in all directions, but somehow I found myself in the saddle. The next moment I was galloping after the field, who were some distance ahead.

Valentine and I could hear the cry of hounds and the sound of pounding hoofs. Soon we had left the copse far behind. In front, sprinkled across the fields, were grey and brown and black and chestnut hunters, scarlet, black and ratcatcher coats, crowned by bowlers and crash-caps, and one solitary top hat; and, beyond them all, were hounds, and still farther ahead we saw the fox for one fleeting moment.

"It's just like a hunting picture!" exclaimed Valentine. "There's something to be said for being behind."

I didn't agree. I was still feeling frantic. It's bad enough being left when you're first whipper-in, but it's ten times worse when you're hunting hounds. I wondered whether we were gaining on the field and I visualised a kill with myself the last to arrive.

We crossed a field of grass and jumped a broken gate; we galloped over the remains of kale recently cut. We seemed to be gaining on the horses ahead. Soon we overtook Harry and the other children on moorland ponies. Harry waved. "Lollipop's going beautifully," he shouted.

The evening mist was thickening. I thought of the long hack home, of cars and gleaming headlights suddenly lighting the silent roads and then fading away again, leaving the countryside to the clop of hoofs and the soft sound of pads on the tarmac. I hoped we wouldn't lose any hounds and that someone would be able to tell us the way to the kennels.

"We're gaining a little," said Valentine. "I've never known the field go quite so fast before."

I thought of Andrew waiting for our return; of the Day's kitchen, warm and friendly and in the dining room the long table laid for tea, with an egg-cup in each place waiting for the traditional boiled egg. If only we can return in triumph, I thought; return to tell of a wonderful day, of a ten-mile point and a run which should live for ever in the annals of the Chill Valley

Hunt. I decided that I must pass the field and be with hounds when they killed, or I would never be able to look anyone in the eye again.

Then, as if in answer to a prayer, the field stopped when they reached a curved line of rails set in a wire fence. I could see them talking to one another before they turned away and rode to the left past where hounds had crossed under the wire.

"What's up?" asked Valentine.

This is my chance, I thought. It was obvious the field had abandoned the rails, though they were not much more than four feet in height with no wire attached and a clear take-off. In front I could hear the cry of hounds growing fiercer each moment, and I knew that they were still running and gaining on their fox all the time. I sent Daystar on as we neared the rails. I heard cries behind and Laurence's voice crying, "Stop!"

But it was too late to change my mind; we had reached the rails. I expected to see a ditch or wire or a warren of rabbit-holes as Daystar took off. What I did see made my blood run cold. Beneath us yawned a gravel pit, deep and treacherous. I felt as though we were jumping into space, that we would never land. I shut my eyes and wondered whether I should ever see Little Hall again. Then Daystar's head seemed to disappear and we landed. She stumbled and righted herself and we were galloping on across soft gravel, with hounds still in full cry in front. My knees felt weak and my head was swimming. I could hear cries behind, and, looking back, I saw Valentine and Laurence, the man in scarlet and a topper, Roger Wilcox and a host of other people gazing over the rails into the pit below.

My head cleared, and suddenly I felt cheerful and reckless. I couldn't resist turning in my saddle to wave to that anxious band. Then I doubled the horn and concentrated on hunting hounds.

Evening and the mist had turned the landscape grey. Visibility was growing worse each moment. Soon Daystar, hounds and I would be cut off from everyone in a world of our own.

In front of us was a hedge, which I examined cautiously for wire, gravel-pits and holes, before I turned Daystar round and put her at it.

I found it difficult to keep near hounds during the next ten minutes. I gave Daystar her head and, oblivious of holes and ruts, I kept my eyes fixed on Vampire, who was still slightly behind the rest of the pack. We jumped a stile and a flight of iron rails, a hedge and ditch and another broken gate. We crossed a field of rough tall grass with a multitude of anthills, acres of plough, a lane, a narrow country road, and countless empty fields of grass. Occasionally I doubled the horn for the benefit of my followers, who I hoped were somewhere behind. Once I counted hounds and found that they were all on but one. I wondered how much time must pass before it would be dark. Then I saw the dim outline of trees ahead. Soon I could distinguish several acres of privet and rhododendrons. I lost sight of hounds, but by their muffled cry I knew that they must have entered the covert. I blew the horn again for the benefit of the field and listened, hoping to hear the sound of pounding hoofs, but all around there was an uncanny silence. Then in the distance a cow mooed and somewhere, far away, a car horn hooted. Never before had I seemed so much alone with hounds. They seemed to have lost their fox somewhere amid the undergrowth. Charmer came out into the open and gazed around hopefully. True Love and Tell Tale started to hunt rabbits intermittently. Daystar stood wearily; she was tired, and I wasn't surprised when I looked at my watch and saw that it was half-past four. Already it was nearly dark.

I decided to take hounds out and ride back towards the gravel-pit. I dismounted and blew "long leave the covert," and gradually my pack came out until they were all on but one, which I knew must be Spendthrift, whom we had left in a covert right at the beginning of the day. I blew "home" and mounted and discovered that my knees were stiff and that I was terribly thirsty. I tried to blow "Home," again, but my mouth had gone dry and I only managed to blow a long dreary toot, which sounded more suitable for a funeral than for the end of a wonderful hunt. Then I saw a splash of scarlet coming towards me through the mist and the gathering darkness. Another moment and the remnants of the field were crowding round me and hounds and my poor weary Daystar.

Everyone seemed to be talking at once. Valentine said: "We expected to see you next in hospital."

The man in the topper and scarlet, whom, I suddenly realised, I had met before, said: "It was a wonderful jump."

"We thought you had had it," said Laurence.

"I shall never forget it," continued the man in the topper. "It was an amazing display."

"We nearly all had heart attacks," said Valentine.

"Hallo," cried Kate, appearing from another direction. "Thank goodness I've found you at last. I thought I had lost you for good and all. Where's our Dad?"

"They did go," said a man in ratcatcher to no one in particular. "I take my hat off to you," he continued, turning on me. "You hunted them magnificently."

I patted Daystar. I couldn't think of anything to say.

"He couldn't stay the pace," Valentine told Kate, alluding to her father. He went home about half-past two. He said Pink Gin had had enough.

It was quite dark now. Suddenly the whole day seemed like a dream. I shall wake up in a moment, I thought, and find myself in bed at home. It'll be Boxing Day and I shall have to hunt hounds, and I shall fail hopelessly. But when I dismounted again and patted Daystar's lathered neck, I knew that it had all really happened. That I had hunted hounds, and jumped rails four feet high into a gravel-pit, and that hounds had run, with only a few brief checks, from half-past twelve until half-past four.

The field were still talking.

"Yes, we're definitely in the East Nightley country," someone said. "That's why she didn't draw the covert. It's one of the rules of hunting: you can hunt into another's country but you mayn't draw." The speaker was giving me credit for something I didn't deserve. It had never occurred to me that we might have hunted right into someone else's country.

"It's going to be the very dickens finding our way home," said the man in ratcatcher.

"I must ask you one question," said the man in the

topper, turning to me. "Did you know the gravel-pit was there?"

I looked at Laurence and saw that he, too, was waiting for my answer.

"Not until I was there," I said. "When it was really too late to do anything about it."

"Most people would have tried to stop then, and their horses would have crashed into the rails and that would have been the end," said the man in the topper. "You rode at them so coolly, we all felt certain you must know what you were about."

"It was a fantastic performance," said the man in ratcatcher.

Kate was standing beside me. She grinned a happy, triumphant grin.

"It was nothing, really," I muttered.

"Home," said Laurence.

"Are they all on?" asked Valentine.

"All but Spendthrift," I answered. "I expect he's home already." There was the sound of clinking stirrups and creaking leather as everyone mounted. Then the man in ratcatcher turned to me and said: "Do you know the way home? We're all expecting you to lead the way."

I had to admit that I was lost. The man in the topper came to the rescue.

"I know the way," he said. "This covert's quite near my home. We're about a couple of miles from Austin-Smith's place."

"Gosh!" said Kate. "That means we're simply miles and miles from home."

"May I make a suggestion?" asked the man in the

topper. "Once I had your box when you didn't need it. May I return the favour today? I have a box waiting for me in Hettington Market Place. The driver will be in the White Lion and I can easily get him on the phone. Will you allow me to lend you the box? It'll take five horses, so I think it'll take all of you and your hounds."

"But where's Harry?" cried Kate. Valentine explained that he and Roger Wilcox and a great many other people had gone home after the incident at the gravel-pit.

Laurence said: "That's very kind of you, sir. It would certainly be a great help." I knew now why the man in scarlet and the top hat seemed so familiar. He had been with us at the end of another great day, when we had met in the East Nightley country and finished in our own.

"Thanks awfully," I said, thinking how wonderful it would be to travel home in comfort; because, although I love long hacks home beneath the moon or in inky darkness, I couldn't bear the thought of fourteen miles or more on weary horses who had been galloping for hours and hours. Following the man in the topper, we discovered that he was called David Peterborough, and later, that he was the Hon. David Peterborough, and would one day own Landsfield Court, a huge residence in the East Nightley country. We followed him across fields, through a farmyard and along a rough, stony lane, to his own house, which was small and white and called The Limes. He gave his horse to a groom and we dismounted and waited, while he telephoned the White Lion and asked the driver of his horse box to call for us. Then we were given drinks and biscuits and slices of sticky lardy cake. None of us felt much like talking. We stood about in companionable silence thinking of the days ahead.

When the box arrived we loaded our hunters and hounds, and thanked David Peterborough, who said: "Not at all," and "Don't mention it," a great many times. Then we were driven away into the night.

For some time we were silent. Then Valentine said: "Won't Andrew be pleased?" Kate said: "Dad won't be able to laugh at us any more." I remembered the twenty-eight pounds, and after feeling my pocket to make sure it was still there, I told the others of its existence.

Laurence, as I had expected, was quite overcome. "Now we'll be able to pay Mr. Day what we owe him," he said. "Oh, how wonderful! We'll be out of debt at last!"

Kate said: "But surely it belongs to Sandy and Andrew? I mean, it was meant for the huntsman, wasn't it?"

"No, for everyone," I said. "For the good of the hunt."

"We've collected lots of new subscribers to-day," said Valentine cheerfully. "I've been an information bureau all day."

"Besides first whip?" asked Laurence.

"As well," said Valentine. "But I must say I prefer being secretary to whipping-in. It's not nearly as nerve-racking."

"We'll have to have a celebration dinner to-night," said Kate. "We can drink the last of the elderberry wine."

And here my story ends. I'm sure you can imagine our homecoming; Andrew, in spite of doctor's orders to stay indoors after dark, waiting for us in the yard; lights; the sound of contented horses munching hay; hot baths, and mugs of tea and boiled eggs. At last we had lived down our mistakes. We no longer cared about the speech on Bank Holiday over the loud-speaker; nor that Kate and I had been lost nearly the whole of the hunt on the day of the opening meet, nor that the Farmer's Dinner hadn't been as merry as we had expected. Our debts were paid. New subscribers would be sending in cheques by every post, and to me, most important of all, I had carried the horn and hunted hounds without bringing discredit to the name of the Chill Valley Foxhounds.

THE END